Fighting
FOR HER
Mate

Fighting for Her Mate

SASSY MATES SERIES

NEW YORK TIMES & USA TODAY BESTSELLING AUTHOR

MILLY TAIDEN

This book is a work of fiction. The names, characters, places, and incidents are fictitious or have been used fictitiously, and are not to be construed as real in any way. Any resemblance to persons, living or dead, actual events, locales, or organizations is entirely coincidental.

Published By

Latin Goddess Press Inc.

Winter Springs Florida, 32708

http://millytaiden.com

Fighting For Her Mate

Copyright © 2016 by Milly Taiden

Cover by Willsin Rowe

Edited by: Tina Winograd

All Rights Are Reserved. No part of this book may be used or reproduced in any manner whatsoever without written permission, except in the case of brief quotations embodied in critical articles and reviews.

Book design by Inkstain Interior Book Designing

Property of Milly Taiden

May 2016

—For my Sassy ladies
May you raise them, know them
& be them. Love you!

CHAPTER One

Night of the scenting ceremony

IT WAS ABOUT damn time her brothers got off their shy asses and claimed their mates. Not that Ellie didn't like the wine and men bashing get-togethers with her girlfriends, but a girl could only take so much stupidity from men. She did love her brothers, but they needed a bit of a push to get them where they needed to be—mated.

Standing on the fringe of the field for the Scenting Ritual, she looked toward the forested hills beyond, while everyone else watched Marco and Kelly center stage. If she and Emma's plan worked as she hoped, all her friends would finally be on their way to being her brothers' mates.

Even Emma had a surprise coming. Emma thought she was helping Ellie with Jordan, Nicole, and Karla mating. But Ellie sent Mason out to where the girls were taping the video for a book Jordan was writing. She wasn't waiting any longer or taking any chances of anything happening.

The situation with the Rahound pack was getting serious. It was best for the women to be mated and for the men to watch over them. The last thing she wanted was for their human bodies to be caught up in a fight with a much stronger shifter. That was one fight her wonderful friends would not win no matter how good they were at defending themselves.

Speaking of the Rahounds, Ellie searched the crowd for her destined mate, Caleb. He was the true alpha of the pack, but his uncle Rocco took control when Caleb's father suddenly died while Caleb was away. Now that Caleb was of age and ready to lead his pack, Rocco refused to step down. She loved Caleb. Had since the moment she laid eyes on him when she'd been a little girl.

But Caleb was keeping her at arm's length, and it started to piss her off. He could do so much with her help. Together they could get his pack back and finally move forward with living as they wanted, as a couple.

In the years under the uncle's rule, the pack had disintegrated into a terrorized community of shifters afraid to speak out or do anything about the abuse they were taking. Now, females from the Rahound pack had been disappearing. It was rumored Rocco was giving women to those loyal to him as gifts for their support. That sick fuck. Every time she thought about how miserable he was making Caleb's life, she wanted to claw his heart out.

They had no proof yet, but Ellie knew in her gut Rocco was committing heinous acts against his own people. Rocco was a crazy son of a bitch willing to do whatever it took to keep power. Caleb had been planning to challenge his uncle for alpha rights, but the timing wasn't right yet, or so he kept saying.

Ellie didn't know the reason for the holdup. But now that a girl was missing from the Wolfe clan, tension was rising, and she didn't know how long her family would stay out of Rahound's business.

"Well, hello, my beautiful lady." A shiver went down Ellie's back. Rocco's sour breath at her ear made her stomach roll. She stepped away and turned to face him.

Steeling her spine, she tried to control the venom in her voice. "Hello, Rocco. What do you want?"

A sleazy sneer spread across his face and his eyes raked down her body. She refused to give him the satisfaction of any fear. This self-control was more than just mental on a wolf's part.

Wolves could smell emotional reactions based on the chemicals the brain secreted. Adrenaline of any kind had to be suppressed. Even if all her animal wanted was to slash her claws across his neck and watch him bleed out.

"I'm just stopping by to say hello and see how you are." His eyes drifted to her chest. "My darling, you are far too beautiful to waste on my nephew. How about you come to the alpha house for dinner. I'll make sure my enforcers are there to watch," his tongue slid between his lips, "over you."

He shouldn't even be there. This was a private ritual, but clearly someone had informed him and he'd taken it upon himself to come. The area was available to all who wanted to wander, but Rocco knew neither he nor his men were guests. Ellie put on a fake smile. "I'd see you in hell before I willingly went anywhere with you."

Rocco chuckled as if she'd said something cute. "You're so like your mother. She was a spitfire, too. Definitely a nice piece of ass in her time."

Ellie gasped then hauled back and slapped him. Fury tensed her muscles. "Don't you speak of my mother or anyone in my family." Her voice lowered to a growl and she fought hard to keep the wolf in check. "Just because yours is fucked up doesn't invite you into ours. We have something you never will, Rocco."

He stretched his jaw, a red splotch forming on his cheek. "And what is that, my nephew's whore?"

She narrowed her eyes. Then she smiled and spoke slowly. "Respect and love from our pack."

His eyes darkened. Ellie smelled his hate as the breeze swept it away.

"Ellie?" her mother called out. A second later, her parents and Caleb joined her. Caleb wrapped his arms around her from behind, staring at his uncle over her head. "Rocco," he said with steel in his voice. "I didn't think we'd see you here." He hugged Ellie a little tighter and kissed the top of her head. "Is everything okay, Ellie?"

She relaxed in his hold. "Everything is fine. Your uncle and I were discussing our packs' loyalties to their alphas. Or lack of." He gave her a little squeeze. She wasn't sure if it was his way of cheering her on or warning her off. Probably warning her off, knowing him. He didn't want her getting involved in anything to do with his uncle or the pack war. Too fucking bad. She was his mate and she wasn't sitting by, letting him deal with it alone. Not when he wasn't alone, he had her.

Ellie's dad and mom stopped beside them. Her dad shook hands with the piece of shit. "Rocco."

He looked her dad in the eye and gave a short nod. "Tristan."

Then he grabbed up her mother's hand and brought it to his lips. The nerve of that sick bastard to touch her mother. "Barbara. It's always nice to see you." His snake eyes focused on her. She took her hand back quickly, a frown marring her face.

Ellie was shocked her dad wasn't all over Rocco, beating him into the ground. On second thought, Dad was sure in Mom's love for only him. As she glanced at her father's face, he seemed a bit smug. What was that all about?

Her father wrapped an arm around her mom's shoulders and cleared his throat. "So, Rocco. Have you noticed an increasing amount of rogue wolves in the area lately?"

Rocco pursed his lips and drew down his brows; a fake contemplation expression if ever she saw one. Whatever came out of his mouth would be a lie. They all knew it.

"Now that you mention it, one of my enforcers may have mentioned seeing a strange face, but nothing other than that. Are these rogues perhaps only in your territory?" His disinterested tone went against the spark of revulsion in his eyes.

Her dad's brow lifted. "Could be. We should all be watchful. We don't want them straying into your area either. With you being the interim alpha until Caleb takes over, we wouldn't want you to have to deal with an issue as touchy as this."

Caleb's body stiffened around Ellie. She had to stop her jaw from dropping open. She couldn't believe her father egged Rocco like this. Rocco shoved his hands into his pockets. The stench of hate escaped into the air. Being this close together, it could've come from any of them.

Within the crowd, someone called out Rocco's name. He excused himself and headed away. Ellie readied to burst. As much as she loved how strong and tough her family was, she didn't want anyone inciting the asshole further. "Dad, oh my god. You were intentionally goading him."

Her mother chuffed. "He's lucky that's all your father did. Arrogant bastard."

Her dad wrapped her mom close and kissed her forehead. "Don't waste mind space on him." He looked around. "Where are your brothers? They need to be front and center to represent the pack."

Both Ellie and her mom reacted too quickly, each starting to talk then stopped when realizing how they just blew the cover to Operation Get the Brothers Mated. They giggled at each other. Her dad lowered his head against his mate's. "Don't tell me. I don't want to know, do I?"

Ellie reached for her mom's hand. "It's a girl thing, Dad. But we promise, you'll be an even happier father soon."

Caleb and her father groaned.

CHAPTER Two

CALEB DOWNED HIS bottled beer in two long gulps, then slammed it against the scratched but clean table at Aric's club, the Wolf Den. Tristan had gathered him along with all his sons for a pre-dinner meeting, men only.

"Hey, go lightly there, Caleb," Aric said. "The tables aren't new, but they're in pretty good shape for as many brawls as they've seen."

Caleb let out a frustrated sigh. "Sorry, man. I'm just so..." A thousand thoughts jumbled in his head, each vying for dominance.

"Let me guess," Mason said, sitting to Caleb's side, "you're worried your mate, our sister, will do something dumb like sisters tend to do."

Aric immediately laughed. "Remember that time she filled a straw with mayonnaise, then stuck it in a vanilla milkshake and gave it to Nate?" Among loud laughs, Nate scowled.

"Yeah, I don't drink vanilla shakes to this day. It was gross. But I got her back. One day when she was gone, I turned all the boy-band posters on her wall upside down. She thought a poltergeist was in her room." He joined the hilarity.

"Mason, do you remember when she put dog food in your Cocoa Puffs?" Jake slapped the table, howling. "I thought I'd pee my pants seeing your reaction."

Caleb asked, "Why would she do that?"

Jake confessed for Mason. "Ellie used to watch some cartoon every afternoon. She loved that show and would throw a fit when she couldn't watch it. So one day, Mason took the remote control and hid behind the couch. He kept changing the channel back and forth until she ran out crying for dad to fix the TV."

Mason laughed. "How did she find out I did it?"

Tristan cleared his throat. "She dragged me into the living room, then picked up the remote on the sofa cushion and sniffed it. She must've smelled your scent on the remote."

Caleb snickered. His Ellie was not just strong of mind and body, but personality and judgment. She stood up for what was right and never backed down when someone needed her help. "And if she were here, she'd kick all your asses for talking about her." The group quieted, the music from the speakers taking over the barroom corner.

Aric tapped his bottle on the table. "Caleb, I hate to be the one to say this, but it needs to be said."

Caleb's body became rigid. Fuck, he'd been waiting for this. Trying to figure out how to get his pack back on his own wasn't working as well as he'd hoped. "Go on."

"This matter with the rogues and vamps is getting out of hand. I'm not blaming you, but the next time Rocco impedes on our people, we're taking him down."

He let out a frustrated growl. "We can't wait for the perfect time, man. Our women have been attacked multiple times, but we can't pin it directly on your uncle, so we're staying out of it until we do have evidence." Aric squeezed the beer bottle. "We know he's a low life, but he's got bigger low lives working for him. We need to catch him in the act and stop all this."

Caleb looked up, a questioning expression on his face. "Who else would do your family harm?"

"First of all," Jake started, "the pack from Las Vegas. We

haven't heard a thing from them, but that won't last. There's got to be some retribution for killing their alpha, even though he did attack my mate." Jake's lips lifted in a slow grin. "I'm not saying Nic killing him wasn't bad, but damn, for her to take out an Alpha after being just turned…let's just say I'm proud of my mate, big time."

Nate chuckled and picked up his own beer. "Don't forget about the Central pack. We took down Lewis Cane and his men when Karla's sister was working with them."

Aric nodded, a serious frown taking over his face. "That's also the pack with the white wolves who attacked Jordan at the ceremony site. But that's been months ago. They wouldn't wait this long if they had issues. They knew Lewis was guilty. Still, we need to be sure."

Tristan looked at Nate. "Speaking of Karla, how are my grandbabies doing?"

Nate's face lit up. "Ah, Dad. They're a handful. But they're so adorable."

"How's Madison doing now?"

Nate laughed. "She can now out-cry her brothers in loudness. I think they're competing to see who can be the squeakiest wheel. If Matthew and Michael are smart, they'll learn quickly to let their sister win. Females are atrocious when they feel slighted by a man for anything."

"If they're like their aunt, then definitely." Caleb gave another sigh. The room quieted again.

Aric looked around at everybody.

"So, Dad. Any reason you gathered us here before dinner? I'm starting to get hungry and our mates are at your house waiting for us."

Their dad let out a big sigh and the boys tensed.

Aric was the first to show his concern. "What's wrong, Dad? You're freaking me out."

Tristan waved a hand and motioned for him to sit. "Yeah, all right. I didn't want to talk about this around the mates because they may get...argumentative."

"You're kidding, right?" Mason said with a grin. Caleb had never seen him this happy until Emma finally mated with him and they became a team. "Emma doesn't have a disagreeable bone in her."

Caleb snorted. Man, he really needed to figure his shit out already. He wanted to have his own home with Ellie. His own family and pups. "Tried talking to your sister lately?"

"Okay, you've made my point." Tristan ran a hand through his hair. He picked up a beer, drank it in two gulps and slammed the bottle down. Everyone quieted at that moment. "There comes a time in every man's life—"

"Whoa, Dad," Aric lifted his hands and sat back in his chair. "This isn't the birds and the bees talk again, is it?"

"Yeah," Jake agreed with a smirk. "You're a little too late for Nate."

Nate threw a wadded up napkin at his brother. "I know where babies come from. I saw the stork land at the hospital with our three."

"Would you all please be quiet and let me talk?" Tristan winced at his unintentional harshness. Caleb watched Tristan. He'd never seemed so stressed to bring up any topic. A round of *sorry, Dad* mumbled around the table. "As I was saying, there comes a time in every man's life when he has to leave home and make his own way." The boys froze, wide eyes on all. He had their attention.

"Especially when all of you are strong alphas in your own right. Each of you are highly capable of having your own pack, if you want to." Caleb watched as the sons squirmed in their chairs, uncomfortable with the subject at hand.

Tristan continued. "Now that all of you are mated, it is time to think about your futures. You probably won't believe this, but soon your alpha side will start to dominate your actions, in part wanting to drive away other alphas in the pack. You lead or let yourself be led, and none of you will let anyone lead you."

"No way, Dad." Aric sat forward, putting his elbows on the

table. Caleb remembered him doing the same thing when they were little kids and Tristan had serious conversations with them. "I'd never make my brothers leave the family."

His dad sighed again. His shoulders slumped and he appeared unhappy with the words he had to say but committed to saying them anyway. "That's how it works, Aric. Whether you want to see it or not. How do you think I became alpha for our pack?"

"Wait a minute," Mason said with a horrified look on his face. "What do you mean?"

Tristan cleared his throat and pushed the empty beer bottle forward. "Our pack was originally your mother's. Her family started it. Have you ever wondered why most of your mother's family is here and mine isn't?"

The boys looked at each other, each shocked as shit. Tristan groaned and shook his head. "This is going as well as I hoped."

Aric sat straight as if he'd come up with a good argument. "But, Dad. The pack's name is Wolfe, which is our last name. If it was Mom's, wouldn't it be her maiden name?"

Tristan nodded, his features still somber. "Normally that is true, if a son of the existing alpha takes over. In your mother's case, her older brother was killed in a car accident."

"I remember Mom telling me the story when I was young and asked about his picture. She said he was driving too fast and his car rolled down into a ravine and exploded. He had his mate with him and neither lived," Aric said.

Caleb stiffened, jerking in his chair. A shot of pure agony coursed through him. All eyes turned to him. "That's basically how my father died. But Mom and he had already split, so he was by himself. It was really late and he was coming back from a meeting. We thought he probably fell asleep and missed the curve, going over the edge. The car ended up at the bottom of hill, exploding."

Jake put a hand on his shoulder. "Sorry, man. Never knew that."

Caleb met Aric's gaze. He was his best friend and only he knew the story, but he appreciated that Aric had never talked about his personal business, not even to his brothers.

"It was so long ago. I don't like to talk about it. I was out of town when it happened. Rocco took care of the arrangements before I could make it back into town. He said the fire—" Caleb paused to clear his throat. "Rocco said little remained to bury. We had a memorial service after I returned." Jake squeezed his shoulder, silently relaying his support and friendship.

Caleb looked up. "I'm sorry, Mr. Wolfe. Please continue about your wife's brother."

Instead of speaking, Tristan turned his eyes from Caleb. The man's expression was unreadable. Almost as if he pulled on a mask. Then with a snap, it was gone.

A waitress set a tray of fresh beers on their table and left.

Tristan swallowed a gulp of beer and continued. "Long story short, your mother became the heir and whoever she married would rule and rename the pack. I moved here and the rest is history." He stood abruptly and tossed money onto the table. "Let's get back to the house. I'm hungry."

CALEB WATCHED TRISTAN closely. For years, Caleb had looked up to Tristan as an alpha role model. His pack loved him and would die for him. That's what Caleb wanted—not to reign by fear and hate as his uncle. He wanted his people's lives to be full and happy. Ever since his dad's car wreck that killed him years ago, he'd only seen his pack become frightened recluses who only came out to go to work and come home.

The children didn't play outside anymore; afraid they'd be kidnapped. Teens, especially the girls, were seldom seen without a group of adults around them, if they even dared to venture out. And the alpha house...the debauchery there. He moved out a long time ago when Rocco started having strange women staying overnight.

For a guy in high school, having so many partially clad women would've been a dream come true. But not for Caleb. His last bit of tolerance dissolved in one night his senior year.

It was homecoming weekend at school. The varsity football team won the game, sporting the best record in the school's history. The school sanctioned dance after the game was wonderful. Ellie was stunning and lighting up his insides with desire and love. He knew he'd marry her not too long into the future and together they would guide the pack as an awesome alpha couple.

Ellie wanted to wait until they were married before they fully bonded. Meaning she was too nervous to have sex. That was fine with Caleb. He'd wait forever for her. The thought instantly turned his balls blue. When it came to Ellie, he'd suffer through anything to make her happy.

At midnight, he had Ellie home by curfew and headed back to the alpha house. He didn't like being there most of the time. Ever since Rocco took over as alpha a while back, the house environment changed for him.

Unfamiliar women stayed the night, making disgusting groans and moans from the alpha's bedroom into the early morning hours. The women were nice on their own, for the most part. But when they were drinking and snorting powder with Rocco and his enforcers, the clothes came off and the fucking began.

Most of the time, Caleb was either in his room studying or

hanging out at the Wolfe's house. Of course, Ellie was there, so that was the only place he wanted to be. This night would be no exception to his routine—*get to my room asap and lock the door*. He'd hurry upstairs and turn the radio on to block out screams of "more" and "yeah, baby."

As he pulled into the drive, he noticed unfamiliar cars parked out front. Not many, but enough to warrant questions about a party his uncle neglected to tell him about. Not that they talked that much. He parked in the garage and came in through the kitchen entrance.

He grabbed a water bottle and winced at the loud music and girly squeals coming from the living room. Of course, he had to walk through the room to get to the stairs leading to his bedroom down the second-story hall.

When he reached the main room, he froze where he stood. Naked skin filled the space. Bodies, arms, legs were writhing in piles of human women; at the bottom of each pile lay a male. He spotted his uncle under five women, all the enforcers, and even men he didn't recognize.

His uncle saw him and sat up, shoving away the females. "Hey, tiger." Caleb rolled his eyes. The man was just disgusting, still thinking he was a male role model, a father figure. "I got something special for you. Come on over here." His words were slightly slurred.

Caleb raised a hand in passing, "Thanks, Rocco. It's late. I'll just go on up to bed."

As Rocco lay back with the women, he said, "I thought you'd say that."

Caleb didn't like the smug sneer on his uncle's face. He kept reminding himself he would leave for college in a few months and never come back to this house.

He opened his bedroom door then closed it quickly, locking it. His finger punched the power button on his radio then a sickly sweet scent hit his nose.

Behind him, women poured out of the en suite bathroom. This invasion of his privacy pissed him off, big time. But he would play the gentleman and not yell or hurt anyone in the process of getting them out.

The gaggle of naked women pushed and grabbed at him. Hands were everywhere on his body, feeling, rubbing, squeezing. He politely knocked away reaching arms, but when one was gone, another took its place.

The women pushed him backward until his legs hit the bed and they shoved him back onto the mattress. He'd reached the point he didn't care if he hurt someone or not. He put as much of his young alpha as he could into his voice. "Out now. Get out of my room."

The women ran for the door. There was a moment of chaos as they tried to unlock the knob, everyone pushing and crowding against the door.

Finally alone, he threw a large duffle bag onto his bed and shoved in clothes, personals, a few pictures of his parents, and anything else he wanted to keep. This would be his last time he'd ever be under this roof—so he hoped at that time.

On his way through the living room, his uncle jumped up, again throwing females off him. "Caleb, stop!"

Caleb's hand fisted as he turned. "I have nothing to say to you except watch your back. I'm the rightful alpha and I will come back to claim my birthright."

Unexpectedly, Rocco plowed into him, leaving a hole in the drywall. "If you whisper a word about what goes on in this house, your mate may find herself in danger when you're not around to save her."

Caleb had the final word with a punch to his uncle's face. He might have been younger and not near Rocco's size, but he wasn't going down quietly. During his four years of college, he never returned to the house.

He stayed at a cabin his father had built for his mother as her private space on the edge of the property. Even Rocco didn't know where it was. Throughout his time in college, Caleb had grown into his body and his animal. He wasn't afraid and wasn't letting Rocco continue to take advantage of his people.

CHAPTER Three

"WHO WANTS MORE wine?" Ellie held a red bottle in the air, waving it side to side. The girls and Ellie's mom gathered in the main house for a bit of men bashing before everyone sat down to Sunday dinner. Man, she loved these women. They were the best friends anyone could ask for. She glanced at Jordan and smiled.

A few years ago, Jordan would've been sitting here mindlessly daydreaming of Aric, now she was mated to him and finally living the happy life Ellie wanted for all her friends.

Nicole raised her glass. "I will. I'm not driving. Oh, wait. I'm a wolf now. I don't have to worry about that anymore." She laughed at herself. "None of us do, right, Barbara?"

Barbara glanced at Karla. "It depends. Has our mama busted out her fur, yet?"

Karla blushed. "Not in the way you're meaning."

"What other way is there?" Emma asked with a confused look on her face.

Ellie laughed. She knew her brothers way too well. They were horny little fuckers. "Let's just say Jake has always been more creative than Mason when it came to their imaginations."

"You mean–" Emma's mouth hung open. "No stinking way. I'm am so going shopping before going home tonight. How late do *those* type of stores stay open on Sunday?"

"The one in the strip center," Ellie's mom said, "closes at six."

Ellie shook her head and closed her eyes. She tried to shut off the image that popped into her head of her mother shopping at that toy store in Vegas. "Mom, I don't even want to know how you know that."

"Please, Ellie," her mom said, rolling her eyes. "Must we have this discussion again? How do you think *you* were born?"

"Mom!" Ellie's hands slapped over her ears. "TMI. I was delivered by a stork. I don't know what you're talking about."

Perhaps it was childish, considering how much Ellie loved

sex with Caleb, but what she didn't want to think about was her parents doing it. Ever. It was easy to be open about sexuality around everyone, but her mom was...her mom. Parents having sex was so...not the image she wanted.

Karla laughed. "That's what Nate always says. He can be such a dunce."

Jordan glanced at her watch. "Barbara, when are the guys supposed to be here?"

"Tristan texted saying they were on their way."

Ellie poured the last of the red wine into Nic's glass, then turned to her mother with a curious look. "Did Dad say if Caleb was coming? Last I talked to him, he wasn't sure."

Her mom gave her sympathetic smile. "He didn't say. We'll have to wait and see."

Ellie let out a long sigh and set the bottle on the coffee table in the middle of the chairs and sofa. Emma eyed her. "Are you and Caleb still having troubles? I thought since you two secretly married—thanks for the invite, there, Ellie—things would've gotten better."

"I thought so, too." Ellie plopped into her oversized plush seat. "But until this thing with Rocco is done, I don't think we'll be normal."

Karla looked up, worried. "Nate has been with Caleb a lot

again hunting for rogue wolves. He comes home every night with torn clothes and scratches on his face. I'm getting worried he may get really hurt one of these nights."

Ellie clenched her jaw and sighed with frustration. "Caleb says he's waiting for the right time, but I don't know anymore. I think he thinks by taking out the rogues, the final battle won't injure as many people. He knows Rocco is taunting our pack, but I don't know why Rocco would want to bother us."

Her mom abruptly stood and hurried out of the room. All eyes watched her walk out then flipped to Ellie.

Jordan raised her brows and motioned with her head toward where her mom had gone. "Is everything all right with Barbara?"

Ellie shrugged. "I don't know. Ever since the scenting ritual, she's been really tense. You'd think having all her sons mated and getting three grandchildren in one shot would have mellowed her, but she's gotten quieter and quieter instead."

"Well, that explains that." Jordan pursed her lips. "I couldn't imagine living with all your brothers after all the stuff that's happened since the scenting ritual. I thought Aric alone would drive me crazy. He's calmed down a bit since getting back from the honeymoon."

Lael sat quietly, nursing her glass of wine. Since the night of the attack behind Mason's bar, Emma had been thinking of a way to include her. On her own accord, Lael was endangering her health by using her Wiccan powers to keep an eye on the future of the pack. When Emma suggested they invite her over, everyone thought it was a great idea. Ellie liked Lael and having her as part of the ladies' night had been a good move.

"I don't think it's your brothers that's bothering your mother, Ellie." Lael's eyes glazed over for a second. "There's darkness in her past the fates were able to save her from. That darkness would have consumed everyone here. Now, it lingers over the pack." Her cheeks warmed and she dropped her chin to her chest. "Sorry, Ellie. I didn't mean to pry into your mother's life. Sometimes my powers decide to do their own thing."

She gaped at Lael. She knew the witch was powerful, but damn, this was something she hadn't expected. Her mother was keeping something from her. "I don't have a problem, but she might. What darkness do you see?"

Lael chewed on her lip. "You should ask your mom. It's not my place. I should not have said anything."

Jordan gave Ellie a glance that spoke volumes and sat her wine glass on the table. "Lael, we can't thank you enough for what you're putting yourself through for our pack's safety. I didn't know what you are capable of and how it affected you until you passed out when Emma was attacked behind the bar." The others agreed.

"Thank you," she replied. "It's my honor to be chosen as the one to protect your kind's species and the role you play in the future." The others sneaked looks at each other.

Jordan repositioned in her chair and smiled at Lael. Ellie knew that smile. She wanted answers. "What do you mean *our kind's species and our role in the future*?"

Lael dropped her gaze to the floor. "I've said too much. I apologize." She looked at Ellie. "How's your training with the enforcer, Mike, coming along?"

Ellie was taken aback at the sudden change in subject. "It's going great. Once Caleb got over smelling him on me, Caleb's been happily pushing me to work with the guy. We're set up on a schedule to train in the gym after the kids have left for the day. I'm definitely more prepared for an attack from any douchebag Rocco sends our way."

She scanned her friends' faces. "You all should get training, too. You never know when you'll need to defend yourself. Especially you, Jordan, since you're the pack's next alpha."

"Yeah, you're probably right. I'm sure me getting more training would only make Aric happy," Jordan said. "But this book on the mating ritual is taking up so much time. After I get it published, I'll look into it. If not with Mike, then maybe a class at one of the women's shelters."

All eyes turned to Jordan with excitement and expectation.

"When do you think it will be published?" Emma asked.

"I need to add some pictures—"

"Oh my god," Emma interjected, "tell me you're not writing the wolf version of the Kama Sutra." The group burst into laughter. If Ellie had wine in her mouth, it would've come out her nose.

Ellie's mom's voice floated into the room. "I heard that. Wait for me before continuing that line of thought."

"Nope," Ellie whispered, "we're changing the topic right now. Not going there with my mother."

"I heard that, too, spawn of mine." Everyone laughed.

Ellie rolled her eyes. "Great." She wracked her brain for anything else to talk about. "Oh, Emma, have Aria and Trevan hooked up yet? We've all seen the looks they give each other."

Emma shook her head. "I know, right? I feel like maybe they need some help or something. They clearly have the hots for each other, but vamps and shifters don't mix. You know the story about Trevan's pack being wiped out by vampires—"

Nicole gasped. "Seriously? Holy crap. Talk about twisted fated mates."

"No doubt," Emma continued. "That's the whole issue. He's having a hard time getting past that species thing. He'd gladly take out every vamp, if someone would let him. But I think he's starting to see Aria is different," Emma said. "Seeing her as different, but her still being a vamp is probably messing with his head and his emotions. I mean, he hates them, but he probably can't help wanting her. I don't care what either of them say, those two are meant to be together."

"Do you think they'll get together? Trevan seems like a nice guy," Jordan said. "That would be some love story. Vampire and wolf."

Emma gave a sad shake of her head. "Right now, Aria is supposedly engaged to the leader of the southern vamp clan. They're supposed to get bonded or married to bring the two groups together. But she never talks about the guy. I've never seen him around. And no one has ever mentioned his name that I know of. Very strange, that group."

Barbara entered the room. "Okay, back to Kama Sutra. What page?" She held up a thick paperback book.

Ellie groaned and the others howled in laughter.

CHAPTER Four

LAEL WATCHED THE women interact. She enjoyed the camaraderie and bond they shared. It went past blood. This family was stronger than anything physical. All was right in the world of the Wolfes, until Ellie's mom decided to share her sex life. At that moment, a baby's cry cut through the air.

Ellie sighed. "Saved by the screaming baby bell. Thank god."

Karla hopped to her feet, as did Lael. "Karla, may I see the babies? I hear they're adorable."

"Absolutely. Come on back with me. We'll see who's fussy. Be right back, ladies." Lael followed Karla down the hall to the new nursery Tristan put in so there was no excuse for his grandbabies not to come over any time.

Karla opened the door to see three sets of eyes patiently waiting. "Well, now that one of you woke the rest, I guess you all want to get up, hmm?" Karla stood at the crib with all three lying in content.

Lael raised a brow. "Is it safe to have all three in the same bed? Doesn't that pose some kind of danger?" She realized how that might come across as intrusive and rude so she winced. "Not that I know; I don't have kids or anything."

Karla checked their diapers. "When we brought them home from the hospital, we put each in their own cribs. And they all cried and cried. Nate and I were at our wit's end. Then, one time, he put them all in one crib to change their diapers and they instantly stopped crying. We figured it was a sibling thing where they wanted to be together. I'm sure you've heard that kind of story before."

Lael nodded. "Yeah, I've seen shows on TV that talk about twins and triplets having an uncommon bond other siblings don't have. It's like they know what the others are thinking or when the other is hurt. That kinda thing. What are their names?"

Karla reached down and grabbed the toes of a little one. "This is Matthew. He's the oldest by five seconds." She blew kissy faces at the boy and Lael was shocked to see the baby gurgle at his mom. Karla grabbed a second little foot. "This is Michael. He's the second baby. And in front of you is our little girl, Madison."

Lael smiled and brushed a finger down the child's bare leg. "I could tell she was a girl, even though she doesn't have any hair like the others. She will be special."

Karla's head snapped up, worry evident in her gaze. "What do you mean by special?"

Lael slapped a hand over her heart. "I'm sorry, Karla. I didn't mean she'd need special care, but that she will be like no wolf in the pack. She will possess abilities others do not. Those talents need to be exercised and celebrated and not suppressed. To stomp out creativeness is to kill the soul."

A relieved smile spread over Karla's face. "I'll keep that in mind." Lael gave a nod saying that's all she could ask for. She reached in and wiggled the feet of the little girl. "They're so cute. Have they shifted into their wolves?"

Karla shook her head and tickled the second boy's tummy. He blew bubbles at her. "Barbara said they won't be able to shift for a while. Something about them being too young to understand their other side. It's like the wolf's soul half hasn't joined yet with the baby's. They have several years to go. Barb said this was a safety measure so they don't accidentally shift and not be able to shift back."

Lael stared at Madison. Worry grew in the pit of her stomach. "Wow, I wouldn't have ever known that. Interesting."

Karla looked around the room. "Do you see the baby bag?" Lael joined in the search.

Lael frowned. "I don't see anything. Did you leave it in the car?"

Karla sighed and caressed the babies' heads one more time. "Apparently I left it somewhere. I'll be right back."

Lael watched Karla leave the room, then hurried to close the door as quietly as possible. She tiptoed back to the crib and lowered the side rail. She laid a hand on the first infant's belly. She had to do this for them and hope it helped when the time came.

"Matthew Wolfe, I hereby grant thee the protection of the lupra gods by joining you and your beast's soul as one. May you grow early in wisdom to start your path toward your destiny. May you live a long and happy life and obey your queen in your mind and heart."

She quickly laid a hand on Michael. "Michael Wolfe, I hereby grant thee the protection of the lupra gods by joining you and your beast's soul as one. May you grow early in physical and mental strength to start your path toward your destiny. May you live a long and happy life and obey your queen in your mind and heart."

When she came to Madison, she went down on one knee. "The Powers that be, I thank you for bestowing upon me the sight and knowledge and honor of blessing our future queen of the sisters."

Lael stood and placed her hand on Madison's forehead. "Madison Wolfe, may the light of the Powers fill you, keeping you safe through your trials and tribulations yet to come. May you grow in the knowledge of your people until the day you bring all into the fold as one family. Listen to your brothers' wisdom and depend upon their strength, for their purpose is to guide you along the pathway to your destiny. May you live a long and happy life and obey the Powers in your mind and heart."

She raised the crib's rail and re-opened the door. Karla stepped into the hall, a large bag decorated with cute baby wolves slung over her shoulder.

"I left it in the kitchen when we came in. I swear I'd lose my head if it weren't attached."

Lael laughed and took a slow breath. "Well, you have a lot to deal with. You're doing a way better job than I ever could."

KARLA SIGHED. IT was always hard to wonder if she could possibly be better than her mother. "Barbara ensured me that being a good mother was innate in most women. I'm relieved she's Grandma. I'm not convinced of my own innate-ness. My mother didn't do a great job while I was growing up."

Lael laid a hand on Karla's shoulder. "You turned out wonderful. You learned to be a great mother by raising yourself along with your two siblings. You know right from wrong and never falter from the path. I *know* you'll do a great job."

Karla held Lael's look until a noise from one of the children broke the silence. Lael smiled. "I should be going now. My bar shift starts soon and I need to get home and change. It's great to finally meet and talk with you. Seems like it's been forever." With that, the bartender left the room.

Karla turned to the silent babies staring at her. She had a fleeting thought that her children at that moment were hundreds of years old, not weeks. A chill ran down her back. It must've been from the feeling Lael gave her. Why did the woman say it seemed like forever since she wanted to meet her? They'd only known about each other's existence for a few years and she'd seen her here and there, even though they hadn't really had a chance to have a conversation like tonight.

Lael also felt certain Karla would be a great mom. She looked at her three children with love exploding in her heart. "Well, cutie pies, I hope she knows something I don't. I'm not that confident. But with your daddy by my side, we'll do our best."

CHAPTER Five

*O*LLIE STOOD ON the back porch when she heard the men arrive. She waited, her mind going through a rollercoaster of emotions. She missed Caleb so much lately. He refused to spend more than a few hours at a time with her. She was tired of it. For so long she'd given him the chance to handle this on his own and she was done.

His scent surrounded her and she couldn't stop the jerk of her heart and the way her animal pushed under the skin, wanting to get closer to his. *Wait your turn, girl.*

She knew what he would do—hold her, kiss her, and probably be on his way. Not tonight. The moment she felt him nearing her, she started down the back porch stairs.

"Ellie?" Caleb called out behind her.

She said nothing, her wolf begging for her to turn and recognize their mate. To spend time with him. She missed him, dammit.

She shoved a strand of hair behind her ear and focused on the trees ahead of her. He was still walking behind her. She could sense his confusion, but she didn't stop.

Far from the house, she stopped at her favorite spot—a slope that lowered to a thick grass patch around her favorite tree, facing a small pond. She stood, waiting for Caleb to catch up.

"Ellie, what's going on?"

He stopped beside her and she finally glanced up to meet his gaze. God, how she loved this man. It killed her not to be living with him. Not to be making plans to have babies and to enjoy their life together. This had to stop.

"Why did you come tonight?" she asked softly, the words sticking to the back of her throat.

He frowned as if he didn't get her question. "To see you. Why else? It's been too many days and I miss you."

She nodded but sensed he held back. "And?"

"To make sure you were safe, okay?" he added.

She turned to face him fully. "This needs to stop. This whole seeing me once every few weeks and then I have to ask my brothers how you are. I have to wonder if you're alive." She took in a breath to lower the anger rising with her panic. "I wonder if you're okay. If you need help, if you need me." She shook her head and glanced deeply into his eyes. "It's not me you should be worried about."

"I'm always worried about you," he said. "You've been hurt before. I haven't forgotten and I won't let it happen again."

She shook her head. "Caleb, let me help you. Together we can—"

"No." He grabbed her hands in his. "I couldn't live with myself if something happened to you while you tried to help me win this war."

She jerked out of his hold and took a step back, hurt and anger pushing words out of her mouth. "So you're okay with this?" she threw at him. "This half-life we're living where I don't see you and we barely speak?"

"Ellie."

"No, Caleb. It's my turn to say no." She tried to get him to see her point. "Do you not understand that I can take care of myself? I've been training, I'm good. No," she rephrased. "I'm better than good. I can kick ass."

He shook his head. "I won't risk it. You're too important to me."

"What about what I want and how I feel?" She stepped away from him. "Don't my feelings count? You're important to me, too." She gulped back the lump growing in her throat. "I don't want to sit by while you deal with this alone. I'm your wife!" She growled when she didn't see his features soften. "Mates are supposed to handle these situations together."

She took another step that pressed her back against a tree. He took advantage of that and shot forward, pressing himself to her front and holding her captive.

"I'm sorry, beautiful." He raised a hand, gliding his fingers down the side of her face in a touch so soft, she almost thought she imagined it. "I love you more than my own life. I'll never stop worrying about you."

She opened her mouth, ready to argue, but he stopped her with a kiss. It started off fast, his mouth pressed hard on hers and his tongue dipped, curling over hers. She should fight the desire to give in, to let go and stop the argument, but she couldn't. She'd missed him so damn much.

With a soft sigh, she opened wider for his invading kiss. The scent of the woods and earth filled her senses. She loved it when he smelled like he'd been rolling in mud. It drove her wolf wild. His hands came up to tug at her T-shirt, the material almost tearing with the force he pulled. He shoved it above her head, the immediate breeze raising goose bumps over her skin and making her nipples tight.

Their lips separated for a nanosecond while he glanced down at her breasts almost overflowing her bra.

"I will never tire of looking at your gorgeous body."

She licked her lips, the taste of him bursting to life on her tongue. "I'm not going to be dissuaded with sex." Who was she kidding? She'd quit the discussion for sex with him any day. His head came down, his lips attached to the base of her throat. Electric tingles raced to her pussy. She raked her nails into his hair, pressing him to her chest as he glided to her breast.

"You smell so fucking good," he growled into her breast. The vibration from his rumble added to the desperation tensing her muscles.

"Caleb, please," she finally choked out. The words traveled up her sandy throat to come out a bare whisper on her dry lips.

He unzipped and yanked her jeans down, tugging the material with enough force to rip it. Luckily for her, he didn't.

He glanced up and met her gaze. "I plan to please you, sweetheart."

She pressed her head back against the tree, her legs going wide to fit his face between them. There was no pause or moment to prepare. One moment he was getting on his knees and the next his tongue was flicking mercilessly over her clit. A short breathless moan struggled out of her throat. Her legs started shaking, but he didn't stop. He pressed into her sex, his tongue lapping at her clit and dipping into her channel to fuck her in quick drives.

"Oh, my god. Oh my god!"

Her hips bucked forward. He lifted one of her legs and placed it over his shoulder. She let go of his hair and grabbed the branch above her head to cling to. Then he cupped her ass and lifted her, giving her the ability to place her other leg over his shoulder and bring her body off the ground.

He licked at her with purpose, his growls and snarls making her more than a little crazy. Her animal pushed at the skin, but this was Ellie's moment. Her time with her man and oh, how she fucking loved it.

Caleb's tongue flickered in quick circles over her hard clit. Her pleasure center ached with her need to come.

"Jesus, Caleb, make me come already," she groaned.

He chuckled into her pussy, the vibration sending her so close to the edge, she took a sharp breath.

His licks on her clit increased, followed by sucking motions and the grazing of his teeth. Good god! She would argue with anyone that those were the easiest ways to make a woman lose her mind. She flew. Her back bowed and she dug her nails into the branch at the same moment her channel contracted around his tongue. Fucking hell, he was good at that.

Her knees were still shaking and her breaths were coming in short gasps when he slowly and so carefully placed her on her feet. She kissed him hard, licking her own body's juices off his lips and getting wet all over again. His hands caressed her full body, branding every bit of her flesh as his own. She was his and they both knew it.

He turned her to face the thick tree trunk. Holding on to the tree with shaky hands, she pushed her ass out and leaned forward, curving her back and offering her backside to her mate.

A soft growl sounded from behind. She smelled how much he wanted her. Fuck scenting it. She heard his need in his breathing, sensed it in the tension floating over her back. He was close to losing control of his human body and letting his animal take control.

She gave a loud gasp when his tongue trailed from her ass up her spine to her neck. He slammed a hand on the tree, his fingers turned to claws, breaking off bits of bark. Oh, yes. He was very close to losing it.

"Ellie…"

She licked her lips and held her breath, waiting and wanting.

Lord, she wanted him more than her next breath. More than knowing there would be a tomorrow. She wanted to hold on to that moment and freeze it in time. The sound of his zipper sliding down and his pants hitting his shoes amped her anticipation. One breath. Two breaths.

He slid his cock between her pussy lips, using her body's moisture as lubricant. "You're so fucking wet, baby."

She gripped the tree, her body practically vibrating with need. If he didn't get on with it soon, she might disintegrate into nothing. "Do you like it?"

She knew better than to ask. He reeled back and one of his hands slapped onto her hip, digging his claws into her flesh. The bite of pain felt fucking amazing. Then he pushed forward, his cock fully embedding inside her, hot and hard, like steel on fire. She squeaked, almost slamming into the tree only to be hauled back into his body.

"I don't like it. I fucking love it. Your," he snarled the words by her ear, "slick little pussy is all mine, baby girl." He licked her shoulder. A shudder raced up her spine. He propelled back and thrust hard, holding her in place so she wouldn't slam into the tree. When he was like this, on the edge with his animal, all she wanted was more. To taunt the beast so he'd get wilder. Hungrier. So she'd get more of that passion he only gave her when he lost control.

"Fuck me!" she moaned. It wasn't her telling him, it was an expression of how torn she felt over how he drove her slowly insane.

"Do you feel that, sweetheart?" He bit on her earlobe and sucked. "Feel my cock taking what's mine?" He bit her. "Do you?"

She nodded.

"You. Are. Mine."

She gulped and continued driving back into each of his plunges. Tension curled around her belly into a tight knot. "Caleb, I—"

"I'm not stopping. Not until your pussy is wrapped tightly around my cock and you're left shaking from how hard you come. And trust me, sweetheart, you will come that hard."

Oh, she knew that was a definite. She mumbled under her breath about him taking too long.

"You want to come, baby. I know you do." He increased the speed of his thrusts. "You want my dick deep and far. As far as I can get. You want my mate stamp on you from the inside." He took a rough breath. "You want me to give you the pups you've been secretly wanting, baby girl." He nibbled on her shoulder. "I want them, too."

His hand curled around her belly, sliding between her legs to play with her clit. She mewled, wiggling back into his harsh drives. More. More. More. She was so fucking close.

All it took was a few flicks of his finger on her aching pleasure center in combination with his deep plunges and she was gone. The orgasm tore through her like a category five hurricane. It left her breathless, shaking and ready to fall apart. Only with Caleb could she open up enough to lose herself in how he made her feel.

She was still riding the wave when he pressed tightly into her, his cock pulsing inside. He came with a loud howl. Loud enough everyone in the house probably heard, but at that moment, she couldn't have cared less.

He sat on the grass with her on his lap. It allowed them a brief bonding moment without being with the others. He held her close to him, tilting her face to meet her gaze.

"No matter what happens, know this: I love you. I always have. I always will. I'd die for you."

She inhaled hard and let her words out slowly. "It is because I love you as much as I do that I would never let you give up your life for me. I'd rather stand by your side and die together. You're mine, Caleb. And I'm not losing you. Not now. Not ever."

CHAPTER Six

ELLIE ENTERED THE kitchen with Caleb in tow. Her mother was putting rolls into a basket with a red and white checkered towel covering it. Her mother looked at her and Caleb's joined hands and smiled. "Good, you're just in time. Wash your hands and come sit."

Ellie's face flushed red on her way to the sink. While he'd diverted her attention outside with sex, her mind was set. She was helping him whether he wanted her to or not.

Caleb chuckled and squeezed her hand. "What are you

blushing for?"

She turned on him with a "duh" look on her face. "Mom didn't need to look at our hands to know we're still together. All she had to do was breathe." He could only smile. She rolled her eyes. Men. "I'm taking a quick shower. Be right ba—"

"No." Caleb squeezed her hand tighter. "I want my scent on you." Her belly fluttered. He held her captive with his dominating gaze. "Besides, it's just your family."

"Exactly," Ellie huffed, "it's my family. I'd rather be in front of strangers than listen to my brothers' smart-ass remarks I know will be said." Despite her words, she loved having his scent on her. Heck, if it were up to her, she'd have him mark her all over. He was hers and she was more than happy for others to know. Others she wasn't related to.

"Nah, they wouldn't say anything," he growled softly, the sound shooting arousal to her pussy. Not good. Not only was she turned on again, but they'd all know she and Caleb were doing a lot more than talking on their walk.

Caleb gave her that grin that turned her knees to melted butter. It wasn't going to work. She propped a hand on her hip. "Hello? Have you met my brothers? Obviously not, if you think that."

He kissed her hard and fast and for a second she forgot what they were arguing about. Then he tugged her toward the dining room. "Stop being so worried. I'm hungry. Let's eat."

They sat and everyone bowed their heads for grace. When the words *let's dig in* were said, hands went flying for dishes filled with mashed potatoes, candied carrots, fried chicken, and hot buttery rolls.

Ellie kept her eyes to her plate, but she noticed the glances and felt the mounting tension as she tried to ignore her shyness. What was she worried about? Sex was a natural part of life. She was married to the man! It was normal to have sex with your husband, dammit! It's not like her brothers never smelled of it. Since the mating ritual, that's about the only cologne they wore, Eau de Sex.

Mason looked down at his plate full of steaming food and took a deep breath, blowing it out with a long *ahhhhh*. "Smells interesting, Ellie. I mean, Mom." The table erupted with male laughter.

She knew it! She launched a piece of her roll at Mason. "Shut it, Mase." She tore off another piece of bread to throw at Caleb for laughing along with them. She was ready to tell him she told him so, but when she chucked the butter-covered goodness at him, he looked up and caught it in his mouth, ruining her comeback while the males applauded and cheered. And somehow all he had to do was give her a single look that told her he loved her and she turned into a teenager all over again.

Her mother smacked her dad in the arm and he covered his laugh with his napkin and cleared his throat. "Mason, apologize to your sister. You know not to tease her."

Mason dropped his fork in his pile of mashed potatoes. "But, Dad—"

Her dad gave Mason the look. "Don't *but Dad* me."

"Ellie knows we're laughing with great respect for her." He glanced down the table at her unbelieving face. "Why should I apologize?"

Their father put his napkin on his lap. "Because I want the same thing your sister got when I go upstairs with your mother later." The room flooded with "ewww, Dad," "TMI, Dad," "I can't handle that image, Dad," "I think I might be sick, Dad."

Ellie couldn't believe he said that, but had a hard time not laughing along with the other women. Her parents were priceless.

Desperate to change the topic, Ellie asked if any plans had been made concerning Caleb's uncle. With the serious issue, the room quieted.

Her mother added her bit. "I think that discussion can wait until after dinner. I think the boys would be more interested in knowing their little sister is now a married woman." Ellie didn't think the room could've been quieter. The proverbial pin drop had nothing on this.

Aric cocked his head and looked at their mother. "*Our* little sister, here?"

Their mother settled her eyes on him. "No, your little sister who lives with the neighbors."

Jake gasped. "We have another sister?" Nicole tagged his arm.

"No, idiot. She's being facetious."

He looked around at the staring faces. "I knew that. I was trying to be funny."

Nate snorted. "I agree with your mate. Idiot."

"Hey," Jake puffed up his chest, "my mate is always right, but I'm not an idiot."

Mason coughed up a sliced carrot. "Dude, you can't have it both ways."

"I disagree," his mother added with authority. "He got it right. And you boys would do good to learn what he just got away with." She grinned at the faces her sons made. "Interesting that your mates didn't tell you anything about it."

Every man turned to look at his mate, but the women continued eating as if nothing had happened. The smiles the women shared with Ellie told her they were more than happy to deal with the questions that would come their way.

An hour later, Ellie and the other women put away the last of the dishes from dinner. Karla, Jordan, and Emma each held a bottle for one of the triplets in their arms.

Ellie looked toward the doorway, then to Karla feeding one of her babies. "Karla, may I ask a personal question that's plagued me forever?"

Karla made a fish face at the baby. "Sure."

"I thought you were on the pill before you got pregnant."

"I was. Have been since graduating." She bent down and kissed the baby's forehead.

Ellie frowned. "Doesn't that make you wonder how you got pregnant? And on top of that, you had *three*."

Karla snorted. "Yeah, I wondered about that starting the day Jordan and I did the double dip."

Ellie glanced at Jordan. "You what? Went for ice cream?"

Jordan laughed. "No, silly. After thinking about the symptoms she'd been going through, I thought she could be pregnant. Heck, I knew she'd freak if I told her to take a test. So I said I'd do it, too. She came to the house with about ten different tests."

Everyone at the table laughed.

Karla scoffed. "It's not like I'd done it before. I didn't know which one worked the best. The boxes all said they were the number one choice. Besides, I was wound up tighter than a rubber band at the time."

"Ha! I knew you would be." She grinned. "I'd do a happy dance if I didn't have the little one here. Woohoo." Jordan bounced in her seat, making her arm load giggle.

"That tells me," Barbara started, "my grandchildren were destined to be born and they thought now was a great time to do it. They'll make great alphas, if the packs survive."

Ellie jerked her head sideways to stare at her mother. "Mom, what do you mean by that? You sound as if the end of the world is coming."

Her mom's features appeared strained. "Of course not. But with all the corruption and killing for power and money, I'm not sure how much longer the hierarchy tradition will remain as one alpha to one pack. Who knows? Fifty years from now, all could be united under one leader."

Ellie shook her head and dismissed that idea. "I doubt that, Mom. But I do see a pack that keeps up with the times to finally let a female be the main alpha and not the husband."

Nicole snorted. "That'll be the day. Men are so arrogant; they'll never give up their 'right' to lead to a female. I'd like to see that."

Michael's bottle bounced on the floor. "Hey, little baby man." Karla looked down at the baby's innocent eyes staring back with a toothless smile thrown in for fun. "Guess you're done, then."

Ellie picked up the breast milk container that had rolled

against a counter. She handed it back to Karla after washing the nipple. "Did you lose your grip on the bottle?"

Karla propped Michael over her shoulder and patted against his back. "I'm not sure. His little arms started flailing and I guess he got his hands on the plastic and flung it away. I've never seen that before."

Barbara joined the ladies at the table. "Looks like he's going to be a strong alpha already." A loud burp came from the infant.

"That's a good boy." Two other burps soon followed.

Ellie stood at the table. "Are you guys ready to meet with the men to talk about what we're going to do?"

Karla set the bottle on the table. "Go ahead and gather the men. We'll put the babies down, Matthew's already asleep. Then we'll join you all."

CHAPTER *Seven*

OLLIE GLANCED AROUND the living room as each couple took a chair. These people were her family. She would die trying to protect them. She wondered at the thought that her best friends, those she met at different places at different times in her life, ended up being her brothers' mates. Like her mom said about the babies, this was destined.

Caleb wrapped his arms around her and she leaned against his chest, she on his lap. "Everything okay?"

"Yeah, fine. I was just thinking about the past and how things turned out for us." He frowned and turned her around to face him.

"Ellie, I know we haven't fully mated, and we agreed on that reason, but you're my life. Don't forget that in the crazy mess going on." The fear for her was real in his eyes and she hated it was there to begin with. "I would walk away from the Rahound pack and become a Wolfe if I didn't know the atrocities my uncle is submitting the pack to. You know I can't let them suffer."

She didn't expect him to and that's what bothered her most. She didn't want him to fight this alone, not when he had her to lean on.

He paused and noticed everyone had taken a seat. "We'll talk about this later." He kissed her like he wasn't afraid to show his feelings anymore. When he suggested they secretly get married, she was all over that in a heartbeat.

She knew her mother was upset with their decision, but she kept her feelings to herself. Her mom had spoken several times about what a grand event it would be when the alpha princess wed. She even had her wedding gown preserved so Ellie could wear it. When she was little, they went through magazines to cut out pictures of things they liked and stored them in a shoebox. She wondered if her mom still had it.

When the room quieted, Ellie pushed away from Caleb's chest. "To be continued later."

She turned to her dad. "You're in charge, unless you want me or Aric to talk." To her surprise, he didn't reply right away. He looked between Caleb and her.

"Being alpha for the Wolfe pack, I will make the final decisions concerning our pack." He paused again. "You, my little princess, are now a Rahound and should join with your mate to care for your people."

Ellie froze with his words. After their impromptu wedding, nothing felt different for her. She slept at the home she grew up in. Still had dinner most nights at home. Still did the same chores she'd been doing since ten years old. They didn't even wear the rings they exchanged, trying to keep the bond a secret.

But now, the reality of their decision hit her in the face. She was glad she and Caleb married, she wouldn't have it any other way, but knowing now her life consisted of different responsibilities and a different role, she no longer felt like Daddy's little girl. She was Daddy's little kick-ass alpha mate. She should get a cape with that on it.

Her father clapped his hands and sat forward in his recliner, bringing her out of her thoughts. "All right. We have several things we need to talk about as a family. A lot of things are coming to a head or lingering closely behind." Jake raised his hand. "Yeah, Jake. What is it?"

Jake cleared his throat and adjusted Nicole on his lap. "Dad, we haven't talked about this and I'm starting to trip because of it." He paused.

Dad pulled his chin in, confusion clearly on his face. "Well, son, whatever it is, I'm sure we can move it out of your way. No need to injure yourself over a trip hazard." Giggles and suppressed smiles broke out. Dad looked at Mom. "What did I say?"

She didn't hide her big smile and loving eyes from him. "Dear, in this case, 'trip' means to freak out."

His brow rose. "I don't get the correlation: trip, freak out. How do you get one from the other?"

She patted his knee and winked at him. "You don't, dear. It's part of the younger generation. It's okay, though, darling. You're not expected to know every term out there."

He sat back, relief on his face. "That explains that." He turned to Jake. "Okay, Jake. What are you tripping over?"

Jake grinned, clearly ready to mess with their dad, but before he did, their mom answered.

"It's trip *out*, dear."

With an angry huff, Dad crossed his arms over his chest. "How do you know this and I don't? I thought I kept up with the young ones' jargon."

"The boys aren't teens anymore, dear." Her mom patted his

thick bicep. "Don't worry. I'll always be here to translate for you."

"Dad, forget about it. What's bothering me is that we haven't heard anything from the Las Vegas pack. We killed their alpha, for crying out loud. They can't just let that go, can they? What about the law on whomever kills an alpha takes their place?"

Aric sat forward and looked at his father. "Dad, if I may?" His father nodded. "I talked extensively with Jaxon about this yesterday. I haven't had time to talk with you all yet."

"Who's Jaxon?" Karla asked.

"Jaxon Gold. He's the alpha for the Golden Falls pack in Vegas. He and his pack were at Nicole's parents' house to help us when Harris attacked. He loaned us some guys to fight the rogues coming here. Great guy. Anyway, he said Grady Harris had just taken the alpha spot. His father's death certificate listed the cause of death as unknown."

Ellie remembered that fight quite well. Poor Nicole had to fight for her life.

Jake snorted. "I bet it should say cause of death: son."

Aric nodded. "That's how Jaxon felt, too. Harris's pack has a lot of money, not him personally, though. Jaxon thinks Harris offed his dad because they found out he'd been dipping into the community fund for his own purchases. How? I don't know. It's all hearsay. But Jaxon did say after Harris took control, the petitions to join the Golden Falls pack tripled in a matter of days."

"Everybody suddenly wanted out," Nate thought out loud.

"Yeah, Jaxon said the reason on most apps was irreconcilable difference or of that nature. I guarantee something was going on, and Harris was the start of it. Jaxon said stay as far away as possible from them. Several of his cronies are still around."

The sound of two car doors closing snagged their attention. Nicole was closest to the window overlooking the front of the house. Moving the curtain a touch, she frowned. "I don't recognize the two guys. They look pretty big. And from the expression on their faces, they're not happy campers."

Shit, what now? Ellie's stomach churned. She had a bad feeling about this.

The men were out of their seats and at the front door in the matter of seconds. Tristan opened the door before the strangers climbed the porch stairs.

"I'm Alpha Tristan Wolfe. What can I do for you, boys?" His sons and Caleb gathered behind him, arms crossed over their chests.

The two men didn't flinch at the aggressive stance. One of the men placed a foot on the bottom step and stopped. "We're from the Las Vegas pack here to talk to you about the death of our most recent alpha."

Jake's mouth dropped open. "Oh, fuck."

Chapter Eight

NICOLE WATCHED BARBARA set a tray of drinks and crackers on the coffee table in front of the two visitors on the sofa. "There we go. Please, help yourselves."

"Thank you, ma'am. The flight here was delayed a couple hours and we came straight here, hoping to finish in time to catch the last plane out this evening."

"Oh," Barbara breathed a sigh of relief. "Then this meeting should be easy since we aren't doing anything radical."

"It should be easy, ma'am. All we need is for Nicole to leave with us." The room erupted into chaos. Chairs flipped back as bodies sprang from them. Yells got louder as each family member told the visitors where they could go. A loud crack of a bone leading into a shift drew everyone's eyes to Jake.

Nicole took Jake's face in her hands and brought him down to her level. "Jake, honey. Look at me." His normal eye color had given way to the wolf's. "Listen to me. Calm down. We're civilized and we will talk like civilized people. No need for a fight. Let's see what they have to say." She took his hand and guided him to their chair. The room quieted and the other couples followed suit.

Under any other circumstance, Nicole might have been concerned, but seeing how the entire family had jumped to their feet in her defense helped her keep her shit together. She looked at the two visitors. "I'm sorry, I didn't get your names and positions within the pack."

The men looked a bit pale compared to a minute ago. But what did they expect? The taller of the two turned to her. "I'm Paul Montgomery, pack enforcer, and this is Turner White, also an enforcer. Are you Nicole Acosta?" His eyes slid down her curvy frame. A deep growl started low in Jake's throat. "You must be Jake Wolfe, her mate."

"Good guess, asshole. Why are you looking at my woman?"

Nic elbowed him in the gut and whispered, "Stop taunting

him. Apologize for calling him an ass--"

"No, I'm not apologizing. Did you see the way he looked–" His face scrunched.

"Jake, calm down–"

Paul lifted a hand in placation. "I apologize for the rude stare a moment ago. I wasn't prepared for someone of your small stature to be the one who took down our alpha."

Nicole elbowed Jake again and gave him a "see, I told you there was a reason" look. She swiveled to Paul. "Yes, it is a bit shocking. But size doesn't always reflect inner strength and determination when it comes to survival instinct."

Paul nodded. "You're very correct. Which brings me to the reason we're here." He set his glass of water on the coffee table. "As you know, universal pack law says whoever kills an alpha male is to take the alpha position of the defeated pack. Since you're a female, that has presented a conundrum for us."

Nic raised her brows. "Let me guess, you can't stand the idea of a woman ruling over you men."

Paul and Turner glanced at each other before Paul answered. "Well, uh, yes. But the pack has come to a groundbreaking decision. Being in Las Vegas, we're very much up with the times of the human world. And it's been decided that having a female alpha as leader is acceptable, if mated to a male alpha."

Indignant heat flared in her face. Her eyes narrowed and she leaned forward in Jake's lap. "Are you actually telling me, to my face, that a female can be your leader only if mated to a male who could also lead? Will said male really be the leader while the female carries only the title?"

She jumped to her feet. "Listen here, you—"

Jake grabbed her around the waist, whispering, "Be calm, remember?"

She fought his grip. "Being calm is for you, not me. I can rant any time I choose."

"That's right! You go, girl." Emma cheered Nic on before Mason could get a hand over her mouth.

Jake had to lift Nic off the floor to haul her back to the chair, but she kept up her fight. "You can bet your scrawny ass, I won't be just a figurehead. I'll be the real thing. Your pack has never been as fucking happy as I'll make them."

Paul looked pale again. "We intend for you to be a real leader. Really. Also, there is a male in the pack who wants a challenge to the death for the position."

The room burst into chaos again. A few of the brothers looked ready to throw the Las Vegas enforcers out the door. The women had gathered around Nicole and Jake, each giving their thoughts on feminism and staying alive.

A loud whistle cut through the air, silencing everyone. Jake raised his voice. "Everyone settle down. As my kick-ass alpha mate just stated this is a civilized discussion. Please, everyone take a seat." Angry faces and low grumbles dispersed to their previous corners.

Jake plopped Nic onto his lap and met her eyes. No words were spoken between them, but they didn't need that archaic form of communication. They were mates with a bond and were destined to be together. The perfect match for each other. Jake gave a tentative nod and Nicole gave back a smile.

Both turned to the enforcers. "Nic and I have come to the conclusion that we will *interview* the Las Vegas pack to see if we're a good fit." As expected, they received confused looks.

Nic sat straighter. "What that means is, there are conditions that must be met before we go. First, if we decide to take the position, Jake will invoke the law for the right of a mate to fight on behalf of the other. That is a must, if we get that far.

"Second, we request the pack give us a few days to meet everyone and talk with them about issues and concerns they have with this whole new alpha thing. They need to understand we're not there to immediately takeover, but to talk to make decisions."

She looked over her shoulder at Jake. "Am I forgetting anything?" He whispered into her ear. Nic rolled her eyes. "We'll discuss that later."

Paul seemed worried at Jake's secrecy, so Nic shared with the group. "He wants to have a guys' night out at the casino." The brothers high-fived and the gals just groaned remembering the last time they were all in Vegas.

Turner, the quiet one of the two enforcers, smiled. "I think you'll make a great alpha."

Nicole shrugged. "Maybe, but that," she said, referring to her answer to Jake, "was based on knowing how my mate acts in Vegas."

Paul set a file folder on the low table in front of them. "Sounds great. Here are your plane tickets for tonight. We'll meet you at the gate." Both men stood.

"Wait a minute." Barbara stood, seeming flustered. "That's it? You're going away? Just like that? When are you coming back?" Tristan took her in his arms. "They can't just leave. It's...it's too quick."

Jake and Nicole shared a look. She gave him a smiling nod. Jake went to his mother and hugged her. "It's okay, Mom. Nic and I are just going to visit. We'll be back before you know it."

His mother sniffled and pulled away. "I know. It's just...you're the first to leave the nest. I guess I'm not ready for it yet."

Nic ran to Barbara and hugged her. She was the mother Nic had gained once she'd married Jake. There was no way in hell they'd be separated for long.

CHAPTER Nine

Ellie came back into the living room with Caleb close behind. After Jake and Nicole left to pack, the group took a bathroom break before getting back into the things at hand.

After seeing the coffee table covered in cookies, brownies and buttery crackers, Ellie turned to Caleb with a sad smile. "I wasn't expecting Mom to take Jake's leaving so hard."

Caleb frowned. "How can you tell?"

Ellie knew this was a girl thing, so she let his manhood remain intact for such a stupid question. "All the snacks on the table are mom's comfort foods. If she had time, she'd make spaghetti."

Caleb was quiet, contemplating. "Is this something I need to know about you before we live together?"

Ellie smirked. "You bet your sweet ass you better know. And make sure to have a supply on hand. You may be dishing out the goodies to get out of the doghouse and back into my bed."

Caleb pulled out his phone and typed, every so often glancing at the table. They made their way toward a living room chair. Mason sat next to them, waiting for Emma. Caleb leaned over and whispered, "Hey, man. I gotta thing you need to know to prevent blue balls. I need to make sure the other guys know this."

"Shit, that's important. What is it?" Mason asked.

"There's this thing called comfort food. Apparently, when women are upset, if you give them sweets and spaghetti, they'll be happy again."

"Seriously? I can do that." He pulled out his phone as Ellie's father walked in and once again, took his place in the worn brown recliner.

Ellie rolled her eyes at the guys' silliness and let out a long sigh. The two guys' eyes met. Caleb mouthed, "What does that mean?"

Their dad reached for a cookie. "That, son-in-law, is how a woman says you're an idiot, but she loves you anyway."

Mason and Caleb typed furiously on their phones. Mason

looked up. "What does it mean when they say *fine*. I'm always in trouble after that."

Aric came in and his brows lowered. "What are you all talking about? This looks serious. Should I call the women from the kitchen?"

"No," universally rang out.

"Sit down, man. This is important," Caleb said.

Ellie laughed at her husband. He was so cute when serious. "I gotta hear this. Keep going, Dad. Tell them what *fine* means."

Her father nodded and winked at her. "Right. It's used to end an argument when she is right, and you need to shut up."

"Oh, crap." Aric whipped his phone out. "I need to remember that. What does it mean when they say *nothing* when you ask what's wrong?"

"Ah, yes," their dad nodded with a pensive look before he once again met Ellie's gaze with a twinkle of humor in his gaze. "That's a classic. It means something *is* wrong and you'd better figure it out fast. Here are some others: sometimes yes means no, no means yes, and maybe means no."

Ellie bit her tongue to keep from bursting into giggles.

"You said *sometimes*," Aric said. "How will we know?"

"You won't." Ellie's father continued. "*Sure, go ahead* is a dare. Don't do it. *I'll be ready in a minute* means sit back and relax with the remote. And if she asks *are you listening to me*, then it's too late. You might as well head for the doghouse with your blanket and pillow." Ellie's dad glanced at her. "How am I doing so far?"

She pressed her lips together to keep from choking on her laughter and raised her brows. "Not too bad. Some could get you slapped. But let me ask you guys what you mean on stuff."

Caleb shrugged. "Sure, sweetheart, but men are usually pretty easy to understand. We say what we mean."

Ellie crossed her arms over her chest. "Oh yeah? When you say you like my dress, that means *nice boobs*." The men feigned gasps.

"We would never!" Nate exclaimed.

"Right," Ellie said. "When I asked if you liked my haircut, and you said 'I love it,' that meant you hadn't even noticed the change."

"Hey," Caleb spoke up, "I did love it." Ellie raised her brows at him. "All right, I hadn't noticed it *yet*. You just got home."

Ellie snorted. "I had been home for hours. We even had supper." Ellie's mom and the other ladies came in, mugs in hand.

Her mom frowned. "What are you all talking about? The men look guilty. What did they do, Ellie?"

"We're talking about what men mean when they say things like *nice dress*."

Her mom handed a cup to her dad. "That means *nice boobs*."

Her dad looked incredulous. "Sorry, dear. I don't mean you, of course." She took her chair. "You ladies know what *let's go out to eat dinner* means, right? It translates to *you don't have to cook or clean the kitchen so we can have sex. Twice.*" The men's eyes widened and they suddenly found the carpet very interesting to look at.

Ellie's dad cleared his throat. "All right, everyone. We still have a lot to talk about and make plans for."

"Hey, Dad," Mason said, "Emma has information from Aria she wants to tell us."

"Perfect. The vampires are on the list to discuss. The issue I have is the vampires may or may not be in cahoots with Rahound. Emma, go ahead. The floor is yours."

"Thank you, Tristan." She made eye contact with each person as she spoke. "Aria attempted a raid on her club to find out who's in charge of taking humans for their blood. When she got there, the club was packed, but everyone was normal clubbers. No human blood was found. Of course, she found Maria in the dungeon, but since she didn't make a big scene, she doubts anyone knew about it at the time.

"She's hoping that means the group has broken up since Anton and Chantal were killed, but she's not sure if there are any other leaders. She's waiting for her 'big three' to return from somewhere. She didn't go into detail about them, so I don't know where they are."

Tristan set his mug on the table. "Does that mean she's wanting to do another raid on the club? Wouldn't the traffickers know she's onto them and move the operation elsewhere?"

Emma frowned and leaned against Mason's side. "I asked her the same question. Since the night we saved the two teen girls, she's had trusted ears to the ground, listening to rumors and taking note of who's doing the talking. I haven't talked to her in a while, so I don't know how that's going."

"What's her deal?" Nate asked. "She suddenly moves into the spooky mansion on the hill after it's been abandoned for umpteen years?"

Emma shrugged a shoulder. "There's not a lot I know about her. Aria's a daywalker, which is a vamp who can take the sun." She nodded at the raised brows. "Trust me, I had a shit ton of question for her, too.

"Oh, and she's not dead because she was born a vamp and not changed into one." Emma grinned. "How freaking cool is that? I had no idea you could be born a vampire! She's a direct descendant from the *original* vampire queen and has more power than made vamps. Her family built and owns the mansion. Why it was abandoned for so long and why she moved in, I don't know."

Mason whispered in her ear. She turned to the group. "I forgot the most important part. She doesn't drink human blood from a human and those in her pack, wait...what did she call it?" She pursed her lips. "Coven. That's the word. They have vowed the same. That's why there's a battle. There are some in her group kidnapping people to drain."

Ellie met Aria. She liked the vampire and knew it was only a matter of time before she and the wolf, Trevan, ended up together.

"Is that why we're involved in their fight? They're taking wolves?" Aric asked.

Tristan stepped in. "Not only that. We have strong suspicions that Rocco is working with stray vamps by providing them victims, especially young female."

Barbara spoke up. "I still don't get why he would do that."

Ellie jumped in with what she knew. "We think he's exchanging victims for the vamps' help in fighting on his side."

"Oh shit." Nate slapped a hand over his mouth. "Sorry, Mom, but Rocco having vamps on his side is some scary crap. It takes two of us for one of them."

"Maybe three of us," Mason tossed in. "I remember how easily the one slashed through Emma." He wrapped his mate tighter and pulled her closer on his lap.

The sound of four car doors shutting snapped up everyone's wide eyes. Ellie got that twisted feeling in her stomach again. Jordan was now the closest to the window, and following in Nicole's footsteps, she peeked at the front of the home, behind the curtains. "Speak of the devil. It's Aria, but I don't recognize—oh, cool. One of the guys is dressed exactly like Dracula in Bram Stoker's movie version. You've got to see him."

Jordan looked back to the room and all the men were on their feet. The doorbell sounded. Ellie's father hesitated, looking at the women. Emma went into action. "Good grief. I'll get the door. Aria won't hurt us." Ellie wasn't sure about the other three.

CHAPTER *Ten*

*E*MMA HURRIED TO the front door. Mason jumped from the chair he shared with Emma, which was normal for the couple. Emma blasted her way through those gathered in the alpha's main house for a family meeting, and Mason brought up the rear to save hers. Emma opened the door, and she and Aria squealed then hugged each other. She'd missed the vampire. With Aria handling her coven, it wasn't often Emma got to see her. The others in Aria's group stared at her with eyes the size of quarters.

Aria suddenly released Emma and stood straight and proper,

clearing her throat. "Emma, these are the ones I told you about. They're among the oldest and strongest vampires around. They are also part of my coven."

"Please, come in." Emma stepped back to let the group enter the house.

Mason whispered as they passed by, "You know you just *invited* vampires into the house. Now they can come in any time they want." She backhanded him in the chest then put a finger to her lips, shushing him.

"I'd offer you a drink," Barbara started, "but I don't think we have your choice of beverage on hand."

Aria dipped her head slightly. "Thank you, Mrs. Wolfe. But you're correct."

Barbara put her hands on her hips and frowned. "Now, young lady, with everything we have been through together, I expect you to call me Barbara." A smile graced her face, showing she was joking with the anger. "How could you think we're not friends by now?" Aria smiled after seeing Ellie's mother's joke. Barbara gave the visitor a hug. "It's good to see you again. We were getting worried something was wrong since we hadn't heard from you in a while."

"I apologize, Mrs...Barbara. I've been doing some house cleaning, waiting for these three to get back." She looked around the room. "Hey, everyone. I'd like you to meet Julian,"—a thin, forty-ish looking man raised a hand in greeting. He was the average-looking Joe who could be anyone in the grocery store— "this is Penelope,"—a beautiful cocoa-skinned woman smiled. Emma closed Mason's mouth for him before drool rolled out— "and this is Zane."

She pointed to the guy in the back. "Please disregard his outfit. He's obsessed with some guy named Bran Smoker." The group broke into laughter, releasing the built-up tension.

The stranger was true to Jordan's description. He wore a silver-gray top hat, coat, gloves, and pants. His hair lay in smooth waves to his shoulders. And the sunglasses perched on the end of his nose resembled John Lennon glasses: small circles that reflected a rainbow of colors like an oil slick.

Zane gave an indignant huff. "Aria, please. How many times…it's Bram Stoker." The man turned to Mason. "If I may be so bold, sir. The *cliché* you referred to—a vampire not entering a home unless invited in—is quite a falsity. I assure you Hollywood does not know the ins and outs of the vampire species. But other than that, I enjoyed the movie."

Emma tugged on Mason's shirt. "What movie?"

Mason grinned. "*Lost Boys*. Don't worry about it. It was before your time. Mid-nineteen eighties."

"I know the *Lost Boys*. Who in their right mind hasn't heard of that movie? Those guys were so sexy." She laughed then glanced at Zane again.

With all once again seated, Tristan turned to Aria, but Aric interrupted. "Dad, may I ask Aria a question first?" He gave a slight nod. Jordan looked at him with a questioning look. "Aria, Emma told us you're a daywalker, so I understand how you can be here. I'm assuming the same is true for Julian, Penelope, and Zane?"

The normal-looking man lifted a finger. "Aria, if I may answer the young wolf's question?" Aria slid back on the sofa and gestured for him to continue. The group's eyes rested on the new visitor. "The answer is quite simple, my friend. After a certain age, the vampire body is no longer flesh as you know it, as long as the body never tastes human blood. Over time, the living cells in the skin transform into a leather-like texture that is not affected by the sun and very strong."

"Wait," Karla barged forward, "what's different about human blood? What do you drink then?"

The male vampire sighed and lifted his nose. "Does anybody ever read anymore? I put all this in writing just for this reason."

Penelope raised her brow at him. "Julian, that was over two thousand years ago. Nobody reads papyrus anymore. You have to put it in a thing called a book."

"Yes, Penelope. Do not patronize me. I know what a book is. Has it really been that long? Seems like last year I scribed the 'pyrus."

"Um, excuse me?" Vampire eyes swung to Jordan. "Sir, I can maybe assist you with that. I'm writing a book on the mating ritual of wolves."

A smile lit Julian's face. "Ah, a child after my own heart." A low grumble disturbed the air. Jordan kicked Aric's shin, but the vampire reassured him. "No worries, wolf. As I was saying, we do not consume human blood from a human. Blood in the body carries a particular enzyme that allows cells to die, be carried off, and rejuvenate; the body is in constant refresh mode.

"This enzyme is quite fragile and the sun's rays easily destroy it. I've seen humans who have spent much of their lives in the sun and their skin is wrinkled and leathery. But as for vampire lore, that is the reason vampires are restricted to the night. The sun literally destroys the skin."

"Okay," Emma started, "what you're saying is human blood carries a cleaning crew. It takes away the old stuff and leaves new. And if you go a long-ass time without blood, the crew dies, leaving the old to solidify in place—the old being the tough skin. So what do you drink?"

Julian's expression became hard. "Packaged human blood is safe. Outside the warm body, the enzyme dies quickly. Animal blood has its own enzyme which doesn't affect human skin. Our resistant covering is almost indestructible. That is one reason why those who make it to this age survive even longer.

"This is one reason Aria has banned human blood. She's doing a good thing for her kind. Yet they cannot control their urges, thusly stay weak. They deserve to die like the dogs they are."

Aria quickly jumped in. "Thank you, Julian. These are our friends who aren't concerned about your past. Let's get to why we're here."

"Agreed," Tristan said. "What brings you to our home?"

Aria glanced at Emma, then Tristan. "I'm not sure if you know, but the first raid I planned on at Embraced didn't really happen. Rumors are flying about why my two treacherous vampires have disappeared. Fortunately, no rumor is even close to the truth. So I think our interference in the trade that night went mostly unnoticed."

Emma's face lit up. "Does that mean we stopped them?"

"No," Aria exhaled a long breath. "Trevan and his guys were given information earlier today about a trade. Their part is the delivery to the club. That tells me now is the time to act." Aria looked to the floor, then met Tristan's eyes. "I'm here to ask you and your pack to fight with us against those who are feeding on humans."

Shock from the question kept everyone speechless. Tristan sat back and steepled his fingers against his chin. "How dangerous will this fight be? Will I lose many members of my pack?"

"I'm hoping to present a strong enough front that they will simply surrender to me."

Julian lifted his chin. "You know there is little chance of that happening, Aria." Julian turned to Tristan. "Reality is we don't know if any minions will stand by the leaders and fight. I venture a guess that most are fair-weather underlings: only around when things are running well. As soon as there is trouble, they're gone."

"Dad," Aric started, "from what we've seen, when vampires have been involved in the attacks on Jordan and Ellie, they ran when help showed up. Julian's guess is a good one."

The vampire's brow raised and he gave an upturned corner of his lips and a slight nod toward Aric.

"Tristan Alain Wolfe," Barbara crossed her arms over her chest. "Don't even pretend to think about this. Not only humans are being taken. One of our own was abducted. And you know as soon as they taste wolf blood, they will want more and more. Fortunately, Maria is young and her blood is not as potent as an adult's."

"As always, my love, you're my perfect mate to balance my alpha tendencies." To Aria, he said, "We'll ask for volunteers who understand the risks."

Aric glanced at his brothers. "You have three right here." He winced when Jordan twisted on his lap. "I know you meant six, my gorgeous husband. If not, you might not make it to the raid alive."

"Jordan, come on—"

"Don't you *come on* me—" Her cheeks caught on fire when she realized what she'd said. It took Aric a second to put two and two together. When he did, he hooted like a were owl on the prowl.

Ellie looked over her shoulder at Caleb. "Don't even think I'm not going." He sighed and said nothing.

Nate grabbed Karla by the waist and turned her to him. "My sweetest love. I know how strong and capable you are when it comes to protecting those you love. So I ask on behalf of the cute, helpless, tiny babies in the other room that you stay with them. Plus, we don't know if you can shift yet."

Karla looked at him with loving eyes. "Of course, I'll stay with the babies. No argument."

Barbara smiled. "Well done, Nate. Was Aric watching you?"

A whiny "moooom" came from the oldest brother's side of the room.

"Everyone settle down." Tristan brought the group back to attention. "Aria, when are you planning for this raid?"

"Tonight."

CHAPTER Eleven

ARIA STOOD IN the shadows in her club, Embraced, a glass of animal blood in her hand. This would finally be it. She'd kill all those who dared go against her. Those who thought they knew better than she did. Vampires she knew were loyal to her mixed in with the crowd. It would end tonight.

Her pocket vibrated and she pulled her phone from her leather pants. A text popped up on the screen: ETA 5 min. The show would start very soon now. She had to make sure the right people were at the club. That meant letting the drop happen first to bring out the big fish, then they got to fry them up. Not that she'd ever think of eating a fish. Something about that thought squigged her out.

Slowly, casually, she made her way toward the door leading to the back and upper rooms. This would be where the action took place. She slipped through the door into the hallway. She passed the stairs ascending to the second level, then put her back to the wall and peeked around the corner.

Several vampires were walking toward the rear stage door. Outside, Trevan and his crew would have the young victims. She didn't have time right now to think about the wolf. Her mind should be focused on what was about to happen, but for some reason she still felt tingles of awareness at the thought of him. Later, after everything, she'd hate herself for spending too much time with him on her mind. For now, she'd ignore the image of his bedroom-eyes popping into her head.

Time for the show. Hopefully everyone was in place. Retracing her steps to the main room, she re-entered the main lounge and headed toward the stage. Her pocket vibrated. A text read: Bait taken. Locked and loaded.

She shoved her phone into her pocket and jumped up to the music booth setup. Grabbing the strung out DJ by the scruff, she launched him forward into the dancing crowd. She found a button labeled "stop" and pushed it. The high-decibel thumping ceased.

The vamps on the floor looked around, like coming out of a daze. Aria snatched up the wireless mic and stood on top of the DJ equipment to become center stage.

"Hello, everyone. Thank you for coming to my club tonight. Here's a couple vampire jokes to get tonight rolling. What does a vampire order at the bar? A bloody Mary. What kind of dog does a vampire have? A blood hound." A male voice in the crowd yelled to turn the fucking music on. Aria raised a brow.

"Hey, dumbass, I said *my* club. Who owns this place?" The idiot paled more than he was. She nodded. "That's right, asshole. Do you know who I am?" She waited for his negative shake of the head before showing off her fangs. "I'm Aria Valderi." She turned back to the crowd.

"No more jokes. They all suck. Tonight's entertainment is a reminder of the vow you took when joining this elite club—no human blood allowed. I'm having a special show tonight, and unless you want your head ripped from your body, I suggest you leave." No one got up. They looked at each other as if wondering if this lunatic lady was for real. They had no fucking clue.

She'd give the stupid fuckers one more chance. With a lift of her hand, she brought the mic close to her mouth. She took a deep breath and yelled, "NOW!"

Speakers exploded, sounding like gun fire, and people covering their ears panicked. The race to the door was on. Much better. Her loyalists gathered the crowd outside into groups to see if any of them had human blood in their systems. It was easy to smell the difference. If they were clean, they were allowed to leave.

Aria jumped onto the dance floor and watched the vamps trample each other to the doors. So far, no one of any importance had tried to leave. Only normal everyday folk. A door behind her closed.

From the shadows, a tall, dark bombshell of a man arrogantly sashayed toward her. He clapped his hands, coming to a stop in front of her. "Bravo, my darling fiancée." Filip was as dashing and smooth as he always was. Under his tailored suit was a body any woman would appreciate, vamp or not.

Of course, the rest of him was damn fine, too. That face probably got him everything he ever wanted. "Here's a joke for you, my love. What happened when two vampires met? It was love at first bite."

"Dammit, Filip. You're doing all this? And I was starting to like you, despite your old, lame jokes. Even contemplated the mating thing, even though it would be a business deal only. Fortunately, that thought wasn't around long enough to make me throw up." Aria winced.

"Oh, Ari," Filip picked at his perfectly manicured nails, "you were always prone to being overdramatic, weren't you?" He softly chuckled. "That's one of the things I loved—laughing at you." His tongue slid between his lips, one side to the other. "And counting the days until I got to fuck you."

"Me? Not a chance, Filip. I've come to take down your operation. Before I kill you, though, tell me why a wolf brings you little girls. Can't get your own victims, Fil?"

She noted his temper kicked in. "Rahound is a tool. You're such a child, Aria. Wait until you get older. You'll see the draw and taste of what live human blood offers. We're not meant to survive without it. We're not meant to suppress how nature created us."

From the shadows behind her, Julian, Penelope, and Zane approached. Filip's countenance faltered just a bit. Zane slipped his glasses off and stowed them in a pocket in his overcoat, then sighed. "Filip, you were always the stupid one, weren't you? You should have stayed in your Turkish castle and bullied the little humans in your commons. You're playing with the big kids now and aren't following the rules."

The same door Filip walked out a few minutes ago opened and many more vampires filed in behind him. "As you see, Zane, I have my own followers, and we don't like you. It's time for the big kids to go as all old things do: into the ground."

Filip look at his large group behind him. "You should have brought along more friends, Aria. Odds don't look good for you."

Aria smiled. "You seem to be missing Anton and Chantal. Do tell, Filip. What happened to them?"

His eyes flashed red, then he threw his head back and laughed. "I should have known it was you when you didn't raise any investigation about their disappearance."

Aria stepped closer to her ex-fiancé. "You've always been too arrogant, Filip. That's caused your downfall. Now, I'm cutting you down to size—to put your ashes into a toilet to send you where you belong. With the shit."

Filip's eyes flared again and his lips pressed together. "I have things to do, little girls to drink. If this show of yours is finished, I'm letting my people take care of the four of you."

She turned and yelled, "Lights, please." The house lamps overhead popped on to reveal scores of vamps and werewolves standing along the back wall, watching intently. A very good-looking wolf stood at the front of the pack. Aria licked her lips.

Filip breathed in loudly. "Really, Aria? You want to fuck a wolf?"

She turned to Filip. "Over you? Absolutely."

Filip's response was instant. He hissed with fully bared fangs, taking a swipe with claws at Aria. She dropped into a crouch, easily avoiding his swing, then launched forward into Filip's mid-section, taking him down along with tables and chairs.

Julian, Penelope, and Zane spread out, keeping Filip's group contained with the back wall corralling them. Several of Aria's vampires came to the dancefloor as well as Trevan, the Wolfe brothers following.

Aria and Filip were well-matched fighters. Her natural power was that of Filip's through age. Still, Trevan didn't look happy. He appeared to be waiting for a reason to step in and tear out the bastard's heart. It brought a slight grin to her face. Silly mutt. He really thought she couldn't take care of herself?

Conversation between the two groups of vamps, those in front of the three old vampires and those behind, turned into yelling, then both groups exploded onto each other. There were more vamp fighters on their side than the enemy's, so Trevan and the wolves were to watch and wait until needed.

Tables and chairs were smashed into splinters and stakes, which would come in handy for taking out a blood sucker who got too close. Half-filled glasses remaining on the tables from clubbers found their way into hands that beaned them into the fighting group.

For a second, Aria thought she smelled smoke. Her quick look around was enough for Filip to get his hands on her and throw her into the DJ stand on stage. Machines and piles of CDs flew into the air, crashing into the stage curtains. Aria rolled to the back wall. Filip was there before she got to her feet.

He kicked her ribs repeatedly. His knee grinded into her backbone, pinning her to the concrete. Fuck, that hurt! Fingers wrapped in her hair and her head slammed into the cement, over and over. She should have been more vigilant toward the bastard. Between Filip's weight and the wall, Aria had no way of getting out of the situation. She flailed, trying to buck him off, but he was too balanced to tumble.

The wolves stood in awe at the back of the room gazing over the dance floor. The powerful three vampires tore through the others like decimation machines set on high. Smoke began to gather above the floor like an inverted fog machine.

Caleb hollered to the brothers and took off for the kitchen behind the bar. He hurried through the swinging door into a blaze that had climbed the walls and burned into the ceiling. On the grill sat an engulfed apron, probably tossed when everyone evacuated. It was useless to look for the fire extinguisher; it was doubtful the fire department could save the building by the time they got out here.

Screams came from the lounge.

CHAPTER Twelve

CALEB AND THE four brothers ran from the burning kitchen at the Embraced nightclub into the lounge area. They arrived to see the ceiling falling through with burning timbers. Caleb quickly analyzed the situation. The group fight had dwindled to Aria's three and a handful of others. Caleb and the brothers urged all non-essential fighters to get the hell out, if they hadn't already.

Mangled bodies lying on the dance floor had caught fire from the collapsing roof. Broken furniture and booths quickly went up in flames. Within a minute, the front half of the building burned around them.

Emma dashed through the door to the middle of the lounge. She took a deep breath and coughed. "Aria! Aria!" She caught a scent toward the stage. She stepped forward then was lifted off her feet.

"Emma," she barely heard Mason over the noise, "what the hell are you doing?" He held her to his body, arm around her waist, feet off the floor.

"I have to find Aria. She's not outside, Mason. I can't let her die in here."

"Where is she?" He squinted from acid smoke in his eyes and looked around.

Emma pointed toward the stage. "I think back there." *Back there* being behind a wall of blazing curtains and stage equipment.

A hot breeze brushed by them smelling like Trevan. He leapt through the stage flames, disappearing from their sight. If anyone were to save her, it would be Trevan. He'd not give up; he'd die trying.

Caleb shouted on the other side of the room. "Julian, did anyone check the back rooms to see if others are tied up?"

Penelope slashed her claws through a large male vamp, slicing him into four sections. She called out, "Julian, Zane and I have these. Check the back." Julian took off with Caleb right behind.

Emma fought in Mason's arms. "We need to help–" Her words were choked from smoke filling her throat. Mason was already on his way out. "No, baby. There's nothing we can do. We can't even get to that side of the room."

Emma knew he was right, but she wasn't the type of person to stand by and wait while other lives were in danger. Ellie came through the doorway, frantic. "Where is Caleb?"

Emma nodded toward the far door. "He went with Julian to see if anyone was in the back." Before Mason or Emma realized Ellie's intentions, Ellie was jumping charred bodies, headed for the side door. "Ellie!"

Mason put Emma down to go after his sister, but a hand grabbed his shirt. "Stay here with the women, Mason. That's an order." Tristan blew past them faster than Mason had ever seen his dad run. Even when his dad chased him after wrapping Nate's bed in duct tape, with Nate sleeping in it.

CHAPTER Thirteen

TREVAN SLAPPED OUT the small patch of fire on his shirt sleeve. Fire meant nothing when it came to saving his mate. He froze in place. Was the gorgeous firecracker vamp his mate? His mind said no, she couldn't be. Not with what vamps did to his loved ones. But his heart said she was not part of those demons. She didn't even drink human blood.

Movement on his periphery snapped his head around. The dickhead with the expensive suit straddled Aria's stomach, his hands tangled in her hair, bashing her head against the concrete.

Aria had her fingers around his throat, thumb digging in to crush his trachea.

Trevan plowed into the man, ripping him away from Aria. No matter how torn he was about wanting her, he wasn't going to let anyone hurt her. His wolf pushed to the surface. He slammed the vamp against the wall. The foundation shook and burning material fell too close to Aria for his comfort. "Aria, get out. This place is about to collapse." She got to her knees, shaking her head as if to clear it.

Trevan punched the dickhead in the face. He knew a single wolf was no match for a vampire, especially one as old as this asshole. Trevan hauled back for another punch when he found himself flying stage right. He landed on his backside and slid to a metal door.

Working their way toward him, Aria and the prick were in the most amazing martial arts fight he'd ever seen. He didn't know anything about karate or the other fighting styles, he didn't know the names of the hits and kicks, but he did know sheer power and the body's ability to do astonishing things.

The two before him punched and sparred and kicked in a beautiful dance from hell's ballroom. Aria blocked hands and legs in a blur of motion. Dickhead sported a grin that waned as the fight went on. Obviously, Dickie wasn't aware how well his gorgeous vamp fought. Reminder to self: don't piss off his beautiful vamp.

Aria drove her foot into Dick's stomach, sending him farther onto the stage. "And in case you're wondering, the wedding is off, asshole."

Trevan pulled to his feet, reaching for her arm. "Aria, let's get out of here. This place is crashing." To emphasize his statement, overhead ropes suspending backdrops burned through, sending lighting equipment and metal supports smashing into the wooden floor.

Metal shrapnel hotter than a cast-iron skillet over a fire pierced Dickie's arms and torso. He screamed and took off running into the inferno beyond the stage. The smell of burning flesh quickly competed with smoke in his nose. He was ready to vomit, which wouldn't be good.

He had a bag of popcorn before leaving for the club. The last time he threw up the little white puffs after drinking too much, it came out a pulpy mess made of a million pieces of the hull. Unfortunately, those tiny parts found their way into his nasal cavity. He was blowing them out for a fucking week.

"I'm not leaving. I have to finish him. He'll just go elsewhere and prey on humans." The stage-front metal light bar support groaned.

"Aria," he had to talk sense into her, "we have the building surrounded. There is no way he'll get out without us seeing him. He has nowhere to run. And if we don't leave now, neither will we!"

She squeezed her fists and blew out her frustration. Trevan was impressed with her lung capacity. He needed to get her to focus on blowing something else. *Shit.* Damn hard-ons.

She passed him on the way to the stage door. "I'll pretend that smell you're emanating has nothing to do with me kicking a man's ass." She shoved her shoulder against the door leading outside, ripping it off the heavy-duty hinges.

His mouth dropped open. Fucking hell was that hot. She looked over her shoulder with a smirk. "And that smell, too."

BARBARA'S INSTINCT TOLD her something was really wrong. Even her wolf paced under the skin. The club's parking lot was packed with vamps and wolves waiting for the final outcome of the fight. Barbara saw Trevan and Aria come from the side of the building. Maybe Tristan, Caleb, and Ellie would come out there, too. She hurried that way then paced at a distance where the fire wasn't too hot.

Her heart pounded. She could barely breathe. *Where were they?* Anger stole her fear. Damn Ellie for going after Caleb and damn Tristan for going after Ellie. *What the hell were they thinking?* Not about those they left behind, obviously. She laid her palm on her forehead and the other on her hip. What would she do if they were both dead?

That thought stung hard. She bent forward and gasped air into her lungs.

"Mom?" Aric and the others hurried to her. "What's wrong? Are you okay?" He gently took her shoulders and helped her straighten.

"I'm fine. Just letting my imagination—" She slapped a hand over her mouth and leaned against her oldest son. When her shoulders shook, he wrapped her in his arms.

"It's okay, Mom. I'm sure Dad and Ellie and Caleb are safe. They're with Julian. He won't let them get hurt."

Her head rolled side to side, but she didn't lift from his shoulder. "You don't know that. What if he left them to save his own skin?" Aric sighed and held her tighter. There was nothing else he could say, not when she was thinking the worst.

Barbara pulled away and sniffled. "He is such a great mate and father to you kids. I'm so glad I married him. I almost made a huge mistake."

Jordan turned to her. "What do you mean? Were you not going to marry him?"

"When I met your father, I was engaged to someone else." The sons gasped at the exact same time, a three-part harmony. It struck Barbara as hilarious that her boys seemed so clueless to anything that happened before they were born. They knew so little about the man their father was before they mated. How noble and brave and strong he was. The extent he went to in order to woo her.

After tonight, that would change. No matter the outcome. Growing up, the kids weren't able to spend much time with Tristan's parents because they were so far away. Plus, with Tristan and his father being alphas, it was difficult for them to take much time away from the packs.

"Mom, we didn't know that. Who—"

"Aric," Aria's voice interrupted them. She hurried over to the gathered family. "I can't thank you enough. I'm glad we didn't need your wolves to fight, but you never know." She put her hand out to shake with the son of the alpha.

"You're a good person, Aria. We'll always be here when you need help. Hope we can count on you, too."

"Absolutely, wolf." Aria was about to leave, but Barbara stopped her.

"Aria, have you heard from Julian or anyone with him? They went to look for prisoners and haven't come out yet." Behind her, the building gave a heaving groan, as if giving its last breath to the sky, then collapsed.

Barbara spun around, speechless, hands covering her gaping mouth as she stared at the pile of burning debris. So many emotions went through her, she felt lightheaded. Aria stepped in front of her.

"Barbara, listen to me." Aria took her shoulders in the same manner Aric had. "If they were looking for prisoners, they were probably at the holding cells in the basement." Barbara wanted to ask why that mattered, but somewhere between her brain and mouth was a disconnect.

"In the basement is a tunnel built for escaping if the need ever arose. They'll be okay if Julian remembers it."

She wanted to scream *if he remembers it*. The life or death of her beloved family members depended on the memory of a three thousand year–

"Dad?" Nate's voice registered in her head. "Dad! Over here!" The crowd rushed toward the small group coming out of the woods. Julian and Caleb each held a young female human. Barbara outran everyone to reach them first. She threw an arm around her husband and one around her only daughter.

CHAPTER Fourteen

KARLA MOVED ABOUT in the kitchen tossing breakfast together for Nate before he left to meet up with Caleb and his brothers. She was exhausted from waiting up last night for him to get back from the raid at Embraced.

She turned to the three adorable munchkins lying in their little bouncy chairs, side by side. They smiled at her, toothless, slobbering, and flailing tiny arms and legs.

Her husband strolled into the kitchen. "Here's my Three Musketeers." He tickled their tummies and made funny noises, creating gurgles from the three.

She noted he wore old jeans that fit him perfectly in the right places and a T-shirt that hugged his wide shoulders. Nate continued to coo and talk in high-pitched baby speak. "Do you smell Mama? I do. She wants to play hide the Butterfinger with Daddy. Coincidentally, that's how you three came about."

Karla swatted his behind sticking up in the air as he bent over the children. "That's not all Mama wants to play."

Nate put his arms around her. "Hey, no talking like that in front of the children." His smile lowered to hers and became a proper good-morning kiss. Toast popped up in the four slot machine on the counter and she pulled away. He pulled her back and rubbed his erection across her lower stomach.

She grinned. "If Papa wants his toast buttered then he better help Mama, or he'll be eating baby food."

His eyes flashed gold. "Yeah, baby. You bet I want my toast buttered. I've got something to spread it with right here." The babies squealed in their chairs. Nate turned to them and she sought out the toast. "Michael's really growing, isn't he? He seems huge compared to Madison."

"Well, Madison is a bit underweight still. But the doctor isn't worried. She said she'll catch up quickly." She put the toast on a plate then peeled off the butter bowl lid.

"Did the doctor say anything else?"

"Nope, they are perfectly healthy." She paused, debating whether to ask a silly question. This was when she really needed Barbara around. "Hon, when do wolf babies become cognizant of the world around them?"

"What do you mean?" He flipped the eggs in the skillet.

"I mean...I don't know what I mean. Maybe I'm just overly worried about screwing the whole thing up."

He set the spatula on the counter then wrapped his arms around her from behind and kissed the crown of her head. "Sweetheart, you're doing an amazing job. Especially since I'm not here to help much right now. The babies are healthy and happy. Everything else we can figure out along the way." He turned her in his arms to see her face. "Tell me what's bugging you. What do you think you don't know?"

She glanced at the babies staring at her. "It's their eyes. They track me wherever I go. It's like one of those photos were the person's eyes seem to follow you no matter where in the room you are. I feel like they 'know.' I expect poetry to spout from them or in Matthew's case, I can see him reciting Einstein's Theory of Relativity. It's a little spooky." She glanced over again to see each child's focus elsewhere—opposite of what she just said.

Nate gave her a squeeze then proceeded to put the eggs on

his plate with the toast. "So our children are way smarter than most babies. I call that a reason to celebrate, not worry."

Karla sat next to him at the kitchen table. "I supposed you're right. Still, I'm immensely happy your mom is willing to help with me all the wolfy questions. I don't know what I'd do without her."

"You'd do great, my love."

Karla wandered into her own thoughts as Jake finished his breakfast. He stood, kissed her forehead, and carried his plate to the sink. "I need to get going if I'm to meet everyone on time."

"When do you think you'll be back?"

"Not sure. I'm guessing we'll check out the club to see it in daylight. Since we'll be with Aria, we might talk strategies or who knows." He pulled her to him and backed her to the fridge where he pressed all of himself along her and took her lips in the perfect goodbye kiss. Damn, she loved it when he did this. But she could kick his ass for leaving her hot and heavy.

A gurgling squeal came from the direction of the kids.

With Nate on his way, she turned her focus to the children. Each were sitting quietly, staring at her. "Okay, you guys. You've been fed and seem pretty content. Do you want to play or take a nap?" She yawned. "Well, you know what Mama wants."

All three yawned, like she had. That was too weird. "Good grief, Karla. Get a grip. They were only mimicking you. That's what babies do." She scooped up Matthew and headed to the nursery. "Let's check your diaper then we can all relax."

After settling Michael and Madison, Karla plopped on the couch and laid her head back. Working as a teacher, Karla was used to getting up early, but now she felt exhausted by nine a.m.

Knocking on her front door woke her. She must've fallen asleep. Sliding the chain lock into place, she opened the door to see an unfamiliar middle-aged guy. "Can I help you."

"Good morning, Mrs. Wolfe. Sorry to bother you. I'm Raymond Sheer. My wife and kids live on the other side of town. We haven't officially met yet so you probably don't recognize my face, but we did see you at Aric and Jordan's wedding."

He was correct. She didn't remember seeing him but in reality, she saw so many new faces at the wedding, she wouldn't remember him if she did. "Ah, well, good morning to you to. What can I do for you?"

His brows pulled down and he frowned. "Oh, Nate didn't tell you?"

An instant replay of this morning in the kitchen ran through her mind. She didn't recall anything. "Whatever he was supposed to tell me, he must've forgotten."

"Not a problem. I do security work and he asked me to come over and keep an eye on your house while he was gone today.

With the rogues runnin' around, I guess he'd feel better if a set of eyes and a nose were outside."

Her body relaxed. She hadn't realized how keyed up she was from everything going on. The fight at the vamp club last night must've unnerved her more than she gathered.

Raymond pointed his thumb over his shoulder at an old red pickup across the way. "I'll either be in my truck or out and about, sniffin' for unfamiliar smells. Let me know if you need anything." He turned toward his truck then stopped and pivoted back. "I hate to ask this of you, Mrs. Wolfe, but do you have a bottle of water I can borrow? I forgot to pack mine from home."

Karla smiled. "Of course. And please, call me Karla. Mrs. Wolfe is reserved for Nate's mom." She laughed. "And even she prefers her name. Be right back." She closed the door then hurried to the kitchen and back. She reopened the door with the chain attached, then realized the gap was too narrow for the bottle to slip through. "Oops. Hold on a second. I need to take the chain off."

She closed the door, removed the chain, and before she had the knob in her hand, the door flew open, pushing her back along with a massive body barreling toward her. She screamed, but the man had his hands on her and a cloth over her mouth and nose in seconds. Her brain told her not to breathe in. Whatever was on the cloth would make her pass out.

But as she struggled, her lungs said something else. She heard a snap, like a bone popping, and an agonizing jab shot through her body. She sucked in a deep gasp as another pop came with more pain. If she didn't pass out from the cloth, the pain running through her body would manage it.

The lights around her started to fade. Her vision tunneled to black and she felt herself fall.

Chapter Fifteen

RAYMOND LAID HER on the sofa. He began to worry if the chemical on the cloth would take effect before the woman shifted fully. After hearing two pops, he wasn't so sure, but it turned out all right. Now for the babies.

HE LAID THE third rugrat on the floor of the apartment across town, then pulled his phone from his pocket. "Hey, boss man. Everything went smooth as ice."

"You have the children with you now?"

"Yep, all three are lying here."

"Can you handle them for a while? Tonya's mom is sick and she had to go out of town."

Raymond's eyes rounded as big as dinner plates. "Sure, boss man. I-I got it."

"Good. You know we can't have nothing happening to those babies. They're insurance. You know what I mean?"

He didn't. "Yeah, boss. I know, I know."

"See that you do. Now, Tonya dropped off a list of things. Like, what to do when the babies cry. What to feed them. She bought diapers, too."

Diapers! Maybe he couldn't handle this. He heard a girlfriend once talk about how disgusting baby shit was. He thought he was going to throw up.

"Raymond, you there?"

"Y-yeah, boss. Me and the babies were just playing. Coochy, coochy, coo and all that." Or was it goochy, goochy, goo. No, his girlfriend wore Gucci, but her coochie was drool worthy.

"Yeah, okay, Ray. And if I call, be ready to off them."

"You got it, Rocco." Ray slipped his phone back into his pocket and stared at the infants. He wasn't sure what to do now. "You babies seem happy. Which is good. I don't want to hurt any of you. I guess you all should just play or something."

Three sets of eyes stared up at him. A shiver ran down his back. There was something different about these babes. They looked at him like he was the enemy. He would swear the biggest one had a scary gleam in his eye, like he was going to get even.

Then suddenly, all at once, they started crying.

"No, no, no, babies. Don't cry. Everything is good." He hurried to the list Tonya left. When babies cry, 1) give them a bottle. He went to the fridge and plucked out three of many stacked on the shelves. "Hey, babes, it's Miller time."

He handed the bottle to the first one on the floor. The boy wouldn't take it. "Come on, kid. Give me a break." Were they too young to hold their own bottles? Shit.

Fifteen minutes later, the three babies sat on the couch--pillows, blankets, and clothes tucked in and around their small forms keeping them upright. He held two bottles for the boys. The female child started screaming. He put down one bottle and held hers. Immediately, that neglected boy started screaming.

He set down the second boy's bottle against his stomach and picked up the first one. The second boy wiggled around and the bottled rolled off the sofa to the floor. Ray let go of the girl's bottle to pick up the one on the floor. She screamed immediately. He wiped the nipple on his shirt and shoved it in her mouth.

The first boy squealed; Ray saw the bottle he held had pulled out, and stuck it back in. The second boy leaned on a loose pillow, rolling sideways onto his sister. Ray put both bottles down, creating instant screaming. He scooped up the roaming child and put him back into the middle and re-stuffed the pillow and blanket between him and his sister. The other two were still screaming.

Putting bottles into open mouths, quietness reached his ears, until the middle boy screeched. Ray looked around for his bottle. It wasn't anywhere. He picked up the kid to see if it had rolled between the sofa cushions. He slid his hand behind the material-covered square onto something squishy. His finger poked it, then he wedged the item between two fingers.

He lifted out a used condom, contents still intact. He yelled and threw it as quickly as possible, not caring where it landed. The two babies still on the sofa laughed and gurgled. "You think that's funny, do you?" He set the kid back on the cushion and re-tucked the padding. All three started crying.

Ray fell to his knees in front of the sofa and pulled at his hair. He took a deep breath. He could do this. After juggling three bottles (he realized he'd stuck the bottle that fell on the floor into the girl's mouth, when it should have been the second baby's, so he took her old one and gave it to her brother. They were twins, they had the same germs, right?) for ten minutes, the children were content.

Now what? He went back to the Tonya's list. *Be sure to burp after feeding.* Okay, that was easy. He'd seen women do this all the time. He picked up the girl and she burped right away. Easy peasy. He had this.

Ray picked up the first brother. He patted and patted and patted. Then instead of the burping noise from the mouth, he felt it come out the diaper end. And come out. And come out. *Shit.* Literally. He pulled the kid away, holding it under the arms, and set it onto the sofa carefully. That would have to wait. Hopefully the last burp will be quick.

"Okay, kiddo. You're the end of this disaster. Let's do this fast. What do you say?" Ray hefted the big boy to his shoulder. "Man, you're heavy compared to the other two. You're going to be strong, aren't you?" In response to his question, the infant jerked, then threw-up a mouthful of milk inside Ray's shirt collar.

The lukewarm liquid rolled down his backside to his waistband. He slapped a hand over his mouth to keep his own throw up from going down the front side. He put the child on the floor, swept the other two to the floor, then rushed to the bathroom.

He ripped his shirt off and shimmied it over his back to wipe off the liquid. Well, it smeared more than come off. Three wails floated from the other room.

CHAPTER Sixteen

BARBARA SET A bowl of potato salad on the dining table followed by Tristan with a platter of rare-grilled steaks. This lunch was heavier than her normal deli sandwiches with pickle spears. But since all the boys except Jake were gathered around the table, Tristan saw a good opportunity to break out the grill.

As Barbara pulled out her chair from the table, her cell phone rang. She hurried to the kitchen and unplugged it from the charger. The caller ID read Jake Wolfe.

"Jake! How's Vegas?"

"Hey, Mom. Vegas is interesting. We've seen some horrible things. If this is anything like Caleb's pack, then you need to get the alpha out fast."

"Hold on, dear. I'm putting you on speaker at the table. Your father and the boys are here. And Caleb and Ellie." Everyone's plate was filled with meat and potatoes.

Tristan swallowed. "Hello, son. How are things there?"

"Hey, Dad. It's surprising, that's how it is. This Grady Harris dude was one messed-up wolf. We've made lots of friends and a few enemies."

"What have you discovered?"

"Harris had his fingers in a lot of pies. Including the mafia. He had a sadistic side I'm not going into. We've heard stories from pack members that make you want to bring him back to life just to kill him again. Painfully." He sighed.

"Do you need to bring in the police for any criminal investigations? I can get with our department here to find out who you need to contact."

"Thanks, Dad. We haven't found anything with solid evidence for prosecution, but I wouldn't be surprised to see money laundering, extortion, bribery, all that."

Mason leaned forward. "Jake, do you want Nate or me to

come down to help out?"

"Or Aric." Aric crossed his arms over his chest, pissed-off expression shining.

His mother patted his hand. "You know you can't go, dear. We need you here right now. You have too much responsibility to be gone." She leaned closer to the phone. "What about the alpha challenge?" She couldn't care less about Harris's deeds. She wanted to know how injured her son may be.

"Oh, yeah. The council here has given us several days to decide whether or not we want to stay. The challenger is Harris's cousin, who the pack thinks would be more like Harris than not. Most here don't want him as their alpha."

"Is it too early to know whether you want to stay?"

"Nic and I talked about that. After hearing horror stories that would rip your heart out, Dad, we realized these people have a lot of healing to do. I think Nic and I can help them get on a healthy path to recovery. But we have a few more days to think about it. Maybe someone besides Harris's cousin will want the position. Someone good for them."

From the far end of the table, the guitar riff for Bad to the Bone played. Nate dug his phone out of his pocket. "Sorry, all." He looked at the screen. "It's Karla. She must've got my message to come over and eat." He pushed a button and a screaming voice blasted from the phone. "Whoa, baby. Slow down. What about the babies?" Nate popped up from his chair. "Are you sure?" His face drained of color. The sounds of breaking bones pierced the air. "Fuck! I'll fucking kill him."

Ellie jumped from her chair and grabbed the phone from Nate as his hand started to crush the casing. "Karla, sweetheart, this is Ellie. Take a deep breath with me. Come on, Karla. Deep breath. Okay, now tell me what's going on. I'm putting you on speaker." Ellie watched Nate pace.

Karla's frantic voice filled the room. "I swear to all that's holy, I'm going to rip this motherfucker's balls off when I get my hands on him."

"Karla, what happened?"

"The babies have been kidnapped. I found a note that says surrender to Rahound or the babies die."

Caleb pounded a fist onto the table. "Too far. He's gone too far. We go to war tonight, midnight." He exploded from his chair.

Barbara picked up the phone with Jake. "Did you hear that?"

"Goddamn, yes. He hurts one hair—"

"I know, Jake. I agree with Caleb. Tonight we fight. We'll call you back later." She pressed the red icon on the screen, then put her face in her hands. Tristan had Caleb by the shoulders, calming him before he left and did something foolish.

ELLIE PUT NATE'S phone on the table and snapped her fingers. "All right, everyone, back in your chairs." The lack of movement aggravated her. "Now, Caleb and Nathan." Eyes snapped to Ellie. They all felt the alpha pull to obey. Caleb stomped back to the table; Nate dragged to his chair. Her father smiled and gave her a wink and a nod.

Ellie remained standing, leaning on the table. "Okay, we need to make a plan. I agree we do something now," she glanced at Caleb, "but I don't know if fight is what we want to do."

Nate pushed up from his chair. "We can't fight. If we do, they'll kill my kids. There has to be something else."

Ellie's finger motioned him to sit, which he did, grumbling the entire time.

"Think, Nathan. Don't react. Emotion gets you killed. How many times has Dad said that?" She glanced at her father; he was serious, but smiling. "Okay, here's a plan. Nate and I will go to the house with Karla. We'll call Officer Barrons on the way and he'll get the appropriate crew to investigate."

Caleb said, "I'm going to the alpha house to confront Rocco."

"I'll go with you," Aric said.

Mason jumped in. "Me, too."

"Wait." Their father's deep voice rang with authority. "Caleb, I respect your position and responsibility, but your uncle has offended *my* pack. He and I will throw down about the kidnapping. If you want to make your challenge at the same time, then we'll be there to back you. Understand, son?"

"You got it."

The group dispersed in the same direction—toward the cars. Aric, Mason, and Caleb piled into Caleb's truck. Nate squeezed into Ellie's car, and Barbara and Tristan loaded into their SUV. From there, they split into opposite directions.

Ellie glanced at Nathan. "Did you smell anything before we got into the car?"

Nate turned to her. "I'm too keyed up. What did you smell?"

"It was like Castor oil or fish oil. I don't know. It was weird."

CHAPTER Seventeen

CALEB WAS SO pissed at Rocco that he would tear the asshole into pieces. Forget waiting for the right time, he'd fight his uncle as soon as he got to the disgusting house. No need for a big to-do with the pack as witnesses, the enforcers would be enough. But they were his uncle's men and he remembered how they participated in all of Rocco's sex-fests at the house. He could see them lying to the pack about the fight or jumping in to help Rocco, cheating for him. *Shit.*

He slammed his fist on the truck's steering wheel. Aric and

Mason glanced at him. Aric asked, "What are your thoughts, Caleb? What do you want to do?"

"I want to kill the motherfucker. What do you think?"

"To be legal, you know you have to present the challenge and have it accepted. If you kill Rocco outside of that, it's considered murder."

"Yes, I know. Dammit." Caleb ran a hand through his hair, then slowed for the sharp turn on the mountain road. "I can't wait any longer. I don't know what I was waiting for anyway. I guess I was hoping for a sign to tell me 'now, Caleb. Do it right now.'"

Mason shrugged. "Maybe the babies are the sign?"

Caleb shook his head. "No, I feel...I feel something important is going to happen. Something that will scream *now*. But I don't know what the fuck it is. It's been driving me crazy. I'm done with putting this off. Who knows what the bastard will try next."

Approaching the next narrow curve, Caleb looked at his speedometer. "Aric, does your dad usually drive this fast? We're fifteen over the speed limit."

Aric and Mason looked at the SUV in front of them and frowned. Aric said, "No. He always stays in the legal range, especially on these curvy roads with steep drops to the river." As they watched, Tristan took the next corner faster than Caleb dared. The SUV fishtailed. Caleb pressed the brake to slow down before turning.

Aric pulled his phone out. "What the fuck is Dad doing?" He pushed his speed dial for his mom's cell.

Before he had a chance to speak, his mother's voice came through loud and clear. "The brakes aren't working. We can't slow down, Aric. We can't stop. Remember what your father told you about the safe and all the important papers. Don't ever forget we love you all."

"Mom, you're talking like—" Aric choked. "Mom, you'll be fine. Dad taught me well. I remember everything."

Caleb thought of his father's death. He died on roads like these, falling asleep behind the wheel and rolling down to the ravine, his SUV exploding to bring his ending. He thought back to the last conversation he had with his father, just before he died.

His dad had the latest cell phone technology in the car so the call played through the speakers. He could keep his hands on the steering wheel at all times.

Caleb was out of town at a multi-day conference for next generation alphas when he called his dad. His father had just left the weekly board meeting, headed on his way home. The meeting had run long, but it was before ten o'clock.

They chatted about Caleb's mother, alpha things, and school. Then his dad was silent for a second then told Caleb he wanted to meet privately to discuss a rumor he heard about Rocco at the meeting. He didn't want to get into in the car but when Caleb returned, they'd go out.

Then his dad asked him the strangest question: "Caleb, did someone have Castor oil in the car?" Caleb didn't even know what it was and asked why. His father said he smelled it when getting into the SUV. Caleb was clueless. They said goodbye and that was the last time he heard his father's voice.

Caleb held back emotions that tried to take him over. Now wasn't the time to lose it. They had another crisis to take care of.

The next curve was approaching too quickly. He felt helpless. There was nothing any of them could do. The three watched silently as the SUV ahead of them hit the rocky shoulder, smashed through the metal guardrail, and disappeared over the side.

CALEB SAT IMPATIENTLY in the hospital waiting room. Aric had been pacing the hall forever. Mason vanished some time ago. Caleb had called all the mates to tell them what happened and to get here quickly.

When he closed his eyes, the horrifying image of the scene flashed vividly in his mind. He wondered how similar his dad's accident had been.

After Tristan's SUV went over the edge, Caleb slammed on the brakes within seconds where the vehicle went over. The two brothers jumped out of the truck before Caleb came to a full stop. He pulled out is phone as he stumbled down the rocky slope toward the mangled SUV and dialed 911.

Pieces of the black auto littered the bankside. The SUV didn't drive over the edge, it flew over. Airborne. Then plummeted to the ground. Caleb wasn't sure, but it looked like the vehicle flipped several times, throwing engine parts and axels and wheels. He smelled gasoline.

All he could remember was the brothers pulling their parents from the wreckage before the explosion. The force of the blast knocked them all off their feet. Thick black smoke filled the air. First responders didn't have any problem finding them.

Time moved in slow motion, yet everything happened so fast. Flashing lights was what he recalled the most. There were so many: multiples of police, fire, and ambulances. He watched as the fire crew brought up Tristan and Barbara on stretchers. They were dead. Had to be. By looking at the SUV, he didn't see how anyone could've survived.

A son rode in each ambulance when they finally took off, sirens blaring. He remained to give police information to start the investigation. He was having a hard time keeping it together. He couldn't imagine what the brothers were going through. Wait. Yes, he could. They would have nightmares like he had for years after his father's accident. Survivor's guilt would soon set in, even though it was illogical. That's what the therapist told him, anyway. Logic didn't work when it came to emotions.

"Caleb!" Ellie's near hysterical yell brought him back to the waiting room. He took her into her arms when she crashed into him. Her body shook with fear and sobs.

"Hey, sweetheart." He rocked her and rubbed his hand over her back. "They're going to be fine. You know nothing like this could take out the alphas of the Wolfe pack. They're too stubborn." He felt her head move up and down on his chest, but her sobs were still there. He kissed her crown. "Let's sit on the couch." He guided her to the worn furniture.

Karla and Nate, along with Aric and Mason, walked in. Mason handed Ellie a bottle of water. Karla asked Mason if he got ahold of Emma. He said she and Jordan would be there soon. The girls would be able to help Ellie, too. Their mates would help the boys.

Caleb watched Karla and Nate. He couldn't believe they were at the hospital when their children had been kidnapped. But then, there was nothing they could do right now. The note left at their house made it clear what was demanded. Plus, they had their cell phones if the abductor called. He was glad they were all together. They would need each other to get through this.

As the final members of the family arrived, a female in scrubs came to the waiting room corner. "Is the Wolfe family here?" Everyone turned to her.

Aric stepped forward. "We're the sons and our mates. What can you tell us about them?"

The doctor didn't look happy. "Both your mother and father were in bad shape when they came in. Lots of internal bleeding, some broken bones. Your father was conscious and able to shift to heal his more serious injuries. He's in recovery where we can keep an eye on him, but he's stable.

"What about Mom?" Aric's words came softly, as if afraid to know the answer.

"Your mom has a major concussion, keeping her unconscious. We had to take immediate action to stop her internal bleeding and brain swelling. Surgery went well, but we're keeping her in an induced coma to let her body continue to heal faster through her other half. We don't want her human side fighting the other side.

"Depending how quickly she recovers, we'll bring her out of the coma as soon as we can. We're hoping about eight hours or so. Then she can shift to take care of most everything remaining.

She's in ICU, critical, but stable."

"When can we see our father?"

"A couple of you at a time can see him. We want to keep him overnight for observation, but one of the nurses said he was already fighting that. He said he has something he absolutely has to attend tonight." The doctor looked around the group. "If any of you can convince him to stay, that would be great. He'll be okay if he leaves, more than likely, but I'd rather keep him to be sure."

Aric nodded. "We'll do our best."

"That's all I can ask. I'll be here tomorrow morning for rounds if any of you have any questions." She turned and walked down the corridor, disappearing around a corner.

Everyone found a seat and sat with their own thoughts.

Chapter Eighteen

*I*N THE HOSPITAL waiting room, Ellie examined each of her brothers to make sure everyone had themselves under control. Especially Nathan. With his babies missing and Mom and Dad in serious condition, she worried he was under too much stress. But all her brothers were born alphas, strong in mind, body, and spirit.

Aric stood and grabbed Jordan's hand. He walked up to the busy nurses' station and asked for Dad's room number. The nurse told him 409, around the corner. They headed off. That nurse picked up files from the desk and headed toward the elevator down the other hall.

Mason glanced at each of the others, took Emma's hand and told the new nurse who just walked in they were going to their father's room. She said fine, and they kept walking like nothing was askew.

Ellie looked at Nate, mouth gaping. Nate grabbed Karla and hauled her to the same nurse and asked for Mr. Wolfe's room. The nurse pivoted to the computer screen and looked up room 409 and Nate thanked her and walked away.

The station's phone rang, which the nurse picked up and turned to the computer, putting her back to the waiting room once again. Caleb nodded at Ellie and they both walked with purpose past the desk and around the corner.

When Ellie pushed the door open, laughter rang out in the room. She shushed them and dragged Caleb in and closed the door. Their dad looked a little beat up, but overall he seemed fine. His eyes were bright and alert.

Aric shook his head. "I can't believe you all tried that. Mom never had a chance when we were all kids."

Ellie's father smiled. "Maybe, but you're all still alive, and so is she." His unintentional pun brought them to silence. Her dad sighed and rubbed his face, everyone waiting for him to talk. "I guess the doctor spoke to you all?"

Aric replied, "Yeah, said you were able to shift but Mom wasn't. But she's stable."

Dad nodded. "That's basically what they told me, too."

"What happened, Dad? The brakes stopped working?"

"Everything seemed fine at first. Then each time I pressed them, they got mushier until they did nothing to slow the truck." He closed his eyes.

Ellie noticed her father's hands fisted tightly. She took one in hers and gently pulled each finger up. "Dad, this isn't your fault. There is nothing else you could've done. You did nothing wrong."

Her dad's eyes snapped open. "No. Something is wrong. Brakes do not completely fail on a vehicle. There are other safety measures for such situations and none of them worked. This was deliberate." His eyes drilled on Caleb. "You've never talked about your father's car accident. I know that was long ago, but was there anything suspicious or strange about it?"

Caleb drew his brows down and stared at the floor for a moment. He shook his head. "Not that I know of. The only strange thing was the question he asked just before we hung up."

"What was that?" Ellie's dad was all ears.

Caleb smirked. "I don't know. Mentioning a rumor about Rocco, and something weird about Castor oil being in the car."

Ellie spun around. "What?" Her fast movement caught Caleb off guard and he stepped back. "What about Castor oil?"

He shrugged. "I don't even know what it is."

"Oh, fuck." Heads turned to Nate. His eyes were on his phone. "Sorry, Dad. Wikipedia says Castor oil is used to make soap, lubricants, hydraulic and brake fluid." Nate looked at Ellie. "You smelled this in the driveway, didn't you?"

"Yeah, on the way to my car behind Dad's. Which means it was on the ground." No one in the room breathed.

"The line was cut? Seriously? That works?" Caleb seemed incredulous.

"There's more to it than simply cutting a line, but that's the gist," Dad said.

"But," Ellie started, "I didn't smell anyone."

"They could've used hunter's block," Aric added.

"Yeah, but who?"

Silence filled the room until their dad spoke. "Caleb, did your father tell you that your uncle was going to marry my Barbara?" Caleb looked at him, astounded, as did everyone else. Ellie's dad smiled. "I guess that's a no." He sighed. "This all started long before you were born.

"Your young father came out to my part of the country for a Next Generation Alpha conference. On my way to the location that morning, I saw a semi tractor's tire bust, making the car behind it take evasive action.

"The car dodged the rubber shrapnel until the end when a big chunk bounced though his windshield. He got to the side of the road safely while others behind him piled up. I whipped to the far side of the interstate highway, avoiding the center lane party. The driver of that other car and I jumped out to help those in the wreck.

"We met up when helping a couple out of a smashed up pickup. I looked over at him. 'Pretty good driving there, mister. You avoided what ten others couldn't.'

"He grinned. 'Just lucky, I guess.'

"We got to talking after emergency crews arrived. I found out he was on his way to the same conference I was. I offered him a ride and he called a tow truck and took care of that mess on our way. We missed the first guest speaker, but hung out the rest of the week. We got to know each other pretty well. Well enough that he asked me down to his home in a couple weeks for his brother's bonding.

"He said a neighboring alpha's son had been killed in a car accident—" Ellie's father came to an abrupt stop and looked at Caleb. Her mate's eyes narrowed.

Ellie ventured a guess. "You're talking about Mom's brother, aren't you? Sure seems to be a lot of car accidents around Rahounds' lives."

Her dad gave a quick nod. "The alpha son's, your uncle's, car was going too fast and rolled down the hillside. So your grandfather wanted Barbara married as soon as she found someone acceptable. As a father, I'm sure he wanted his daughter to find her true mate and marry for love, but time wasn't in their favor, and she understood that.

"Rocco had been after Barbara for years. Your mom said even though he was ten years older than her, he always seemed to be where she was with her high school friends. He never seemed to notice her, she thought, but he was always around. She laughed it off and thought it kind of romantic. Like he was a guardian angel."

Caleb snorted. "More like a guardian demon." Ellie's dad had a partial smile.

Her dad continued. "So when Barbara's brother was killed, Rocco was right there to give a shoulder to the family, and especially Barbara. So, it was no surprise to your mother when Rocco said he'd gladly marry her.

"Your mother didn't love him. Didn't even know him, except for his face and whose pack he belonged to. But after several get-togethers and scenting ceremonies with other packs and no mate prospects that stuck around–"

"What do you mean by that, Dad?" Mason asked. Their dad was quiet a minute, lost in his own thoughts. Then he looked up.

"Now that I'm seeing this at a new perspective, it sorta makes sense. As you know, your mother is a beautiful person, inside and out. It should've been extremely easy to find someone interested in her. But after a first date, seems the young men never asked for a second. Or they did, but never called again. I never thought about it, but they could've had some outside influence telling them to stay away."

By the anger scent filling the room, Ellie noted everyone was catching on to the point of the story—Rocco.

"But for his part in that," her dad started, "I would have to thank Rocco for his interference. And then getting Barbara to agree to marrying him to stop others from coming around."

"How did you meet Mom then, Dad?"

"Well, as mentioned earlier, Caleb's father asked me down for the wedding. They had no contacts in my part of the country and my family had none here. So it was diplomatically, as well as socially, a good thing for me to visit and meet new allies.

"I arrive on that Friday with the ceremony on Sunday. I would stay at the alpha house and hang out with the men in the groom's party." He gave a little laugh then grabbed his sore ribs and lay back in the hospital bed. "That's a weekend I'll never forget." He closed his eyes and replayed it all as he told the story to his kids...

CHAPTER Nineteen

AS SOON AS the young Tristan stepped out of the truck inside the Rahound alpha's garage, he knew something was different. His wolf ran crazy in his head. It breathed heavily enough to hyperventilate if it was in its form instead of the human side. Tristan had no clue what the hell the nutso wolf was doing.

Conly looked at Tristan from the other side of the truck. "You okay, man? You look sick."

Tristan got ahold of himself. "Yeah, fine. My wolf is going crazy for some reason."

Conly frowned, but didn't say anything. He continued toward the garage door to the house. "I almost forgot. The ladies in the bride's party are throwing a bridal shower for my brother's soon-to-be mate." He winked. "Maybe you'll catch the eye of a dish to eat tonight. I think that's what your wolf is smelling–a mate."

Tristan laughed. "Well, I hope the wolf's not right, but eating something furry tonight would be nice." The men laughed over the male-bonding tawdriness. Conly opened the kitchen door, letting all the women's chatter seep out.

Tristan stepped into the kitchen and froze. The most beautiful woman he'd ever seen stood among the crowd. Her face glowed like an angel, her smile lighting her eyes. He couldn't see her body through the mass of people, but that didn't matter too much. He'd love her even if she was skinny. His mama's cooking would make her fill out to the lushness he desired in women. No bag of bones for him.

Standing next to him, he heard Conly talking up a quiet storm. "Of all the motherfucking…why the fucking hell…now of all goddamn times…"

Tristan didn't take his eyes from the woman, who tilted her nose to the air, taking small sniffs. "Conly, who's that stunning angel–"

Conly grabbed his arm and dragged him through the kitchen as the woman caught Tristan's look. Their eyes locked and he knew he'd found his mate. And the wolf agreed, wholeheartedly. He tried to knock Conly's grip from his wrist.

"Conly, man. Let go. I've found my mate. Can you believe it?" Sheer joy spread through Tristan, a peace he'd never known.

"Goddammit, Tristan. You've fucked up this entire thing." He continued to mutter to himself, "...of all mother—" and dragged Tristan down the hall.

Tristan was tempted to ignore Conly and take him down if he didn't concede. "Conly, dude, you're starting to piss me off. Let go."

Conly slung him into the den and slammed the door behind them. "And you've already pissed me off."

Tristan's eyes popped innocently wide and his mouth fell open. "Me? I just got here. What the fuck's with you?" A soft knock snapped both their heads around. He started to move for the entrance.

"Don't move, Wolfe. I'll get the door." Conly opened the door to the sight of Tristan's mate. She was even more enchanting up close. They stood motionless, eyes once again locked.

Conly sighed. "Tristan, meet Barbara, my brother's soon-to-be wife."

Now Tristan understood what the fuck was up. "Oh."

Barbara stepped into the room, eyes remaining fixed on Tristan, and Conly closed the door. "Fuck. *I'm* not explaining this to Mom and Dad." He paced, almost frantically. Tristan chose to ignore him and focus on the rest of his life. He reached out a hand to her.

He brought her hand to his lips and he kissed each knuckle. Conly groaned in the background. Tristan held her hand, each staring. His wolf said introduce yourself, dumbass—stick your nose in her crotch.

In his head, Tristan frowned at his animal. I don't stick my nose in her crotch, unless I want to get slapped, idiot animal. Good thing I'm in charge—

"Hi, I'm Barbara. Conly said you're Tristan."

Tristan thought he'd wow her with smooth talk and suave moves, but what came out of his mouth was "Yeah." Well, fuck, wasn't he the idiot now. He lifted her hand to his nose. She covered her smile with her other hand.

"Tristan," her voice was a lullaby, "would you like to sit."

"Yeah." He'd gladly float wherever she wanted to go. Sit, stand, stay. He didn't care. As long as she was with him.

She nodded with a grin. "How about something to drink"

"Yeah." He'd parch her thirst in any way he could. She was so beautiful. He'd do anything for her.

"Conly is naked and running around the room."

"Yeah." She was so beautiful. Her words made an image in his head. "Wait, what?" A growl erupted from his chest. She didn't need to be looking at other naked men. Only him. He stood from a sofa he didn't remember sitting on.

Conly stared at them, arms crossed over her chest. "Tristan." He sounded exasperated. Then his arms stretched toward her. "Barb, what now? You can't just go out there and cancel the joining. We've got people coming in from all over. Not to mention your side of the family is already here."

She turned to Tristan. "All my family has arrived. How soon can your parents be here?"

CHAPTER Twenty

*A*LL THE WOLFE kids, except Jake in Las Vegas, remained in shock after their father was done telling his story. Ellie retained her sense first. "Wow, Dad. I can see Rocco being really mad at you and Mom. I bet that was a bit awkward, having to tell the parents and family. Obviously, you did."

"We did, and yes, it was awkward. But most of them were happy for us. Back then, finding your mate was much rarer than nowadays when young people can travel greater distances with ease and socialize with more groups. Not to mention all the online stuff."

Caleb ran a hand through his hair, his arm wrapping around Ellie. "That seals it for me. Seems my uncle hasn't changed his M.O." Ellie watched as anger took over his scent.

She took his hands into hers. "Caleb, whatever you decide, I'll back you. I trust you to be honest and good. I know you'll make the right decision. True born alphas always do." His eyes met hers. She saw so much love, trust, and appreciation aimed at her, she almost wanted to cry. This was her mate. And now after hearing her dad's story, she was more than convinced they were meant to be together.

He kissed her then pulled back and leaned his forehead against hers. "I'm taking him down for you and me. Taking him down for your parents. Down for your mother's brother. And most importantly, for my father." She slid her arms around his neck and held him tightly, knowing what was happening tonight. Someone would die.

Aric cleared his throat. "Caleb, whatever you want to do, I'm behind you all the way. And if you know now isn't the time, then I say it is for me and my brothers. And the babies. I'll take him in an alpha challenge, seeing as I'm temporarily in charge until Dad is out of the hospital."

His father flashed him an angry look. "I'm not—"

"You're in the hospital, Dad. You were almost fucking dead a few hours ago. The doctor wants to keep you overnight and you're staying—"

Their father pulled himself straighter in bed with a slight wince. "I'm perfectly—"

"Dad," Ellie started, "who's going to be here when Mom wakes up? Dad, we're going to stand up to a bully who needs a lesson in humility. You taught us to protect the family, love the family, and that's what we're here to do. You and Mom raised us right. It's time we showed you what you've reaped."

Her dad held tears back in his proud eyes. "I must say, the youngest of all has grown into a force to be reckoned with. Which must mean the rest of you are no longer boys, even though you will always be that to your mother and me. I will be here when your mother wakes later. Now, go do what you have to."

"Thanks, Dad." Everyone moved toward the door. Aric pulled his buzzing phone from his pocket. "Yeah, this is Aric Wolfe. How can I help you?"

"I'm calling on behalf of the wolf council for the Central pack." All wolf ears in the room heard both sides of the conversation and stopped. "We need to talk with your alpha about the death of ours. And the son, Mason Wolfe."

Aric dropped his head into his hand. "Fuck."

Chapter Twenty One

OLLIE SAT QUIETLY in the front passenger seat of Caleb's truck listening to Aric as he told the group about the Central Pack dilemma. They were headed to the Rahound alpha house to confront Rocco.

"Lewis tried to take Jordan because she killed the white wolf who happened to be Lewis's sister."

"It was self-defense," Jordan added. "The bitch would've killed me if I hadn't taken her out first."

Aric kissed his mate's forehead. "I know, sweetheart. You're total alpha female. But that was Lewis's excuse for being here and hurting you."

Mason said, "So how does that pertain to me?"

Aric wiped a hand down his face. "All right, keep up with me. Not sure if I'll get it right again." He held up a finger. "Lewis's sister attacked Jordan because Jordan is my mate and his sister wanted an alpha. Jordan's self-defense took out the woman. Lewis wanted retribution for his sister, but his alpha father said there would be no consequences since his daughter struck first. Lewis didn't like that so he killed his father and took over the alpha position and came after Jordan.

"After Nate and I took out Lewis and his second-in-command, that left only the widow. The council is demanding one of the unmarried alpha Wolfe sons marry the widow and resume the position."

"But," Emma growled, "Mason is already married to me."

Ellie joined in at that point. "Oh, yeah. Thanks for the wedding invite, Em."

"I know. It looked just like yours," Emma hollered. They both laughed, knowing Ellie didn't send out invites when she and Caleb secretly married. She looked to Aric. "Sorry, you may continue now."

The eldest brother raised a brow at her haughtiness. Emma rolled her eyes. "I'm kidding, Your Behind-ness." The girls laughed again. Ellie suspected poor Aric thought he'd never get respect from any of the mates in the group. But it was the opposite actually.

Aric pressed his lips together, then continued a moment later. "The Central pack investigated public records to see who of the brothers wasn't married and they didn't find a certificate for Mason. They want him to marry the widow."

"But that doesn't make sense. The JP married us personally," Mason said.

"Hey, Mason," Caleb called from the front, "what's the name of the JP?"

Mason looked at Emma. "His last name began with an *R*. Roner or Rinert."

"Rineheart," Emma said. Mason agreed.

Caleb shook his head. "He was part of my pack. He died of a stroke." He thumped his fingers on the steering wheel. "When were you married?"

Emma glanced at Caleb. "Not too long ago. When did he die?"

Caleb grunted. "Not too long ago."

"But he married us," Mason explained.

"Maybe he died before he filed the marriage certificate," Caleb said.

Emma stared at Mason with horror on her face. "Does that

mean we're not legally married?"

"It's the 50-50-90 rule," Aric said.

Mason scrunched his face. "What the hell are you talking about?"

"Anytime you have a 50-50 chance of getting something right," Aric started, "there's a ninety percent probability you'll get it wrong."

"You're not helping." Emma scowled.

Ellie's gut twisted as she watched the late afternoon sun sink.

Finally, Aric looked around. "Listen, everybody. We'll worry about it later. We're almost to the Rahound alpha house. Caleb, you have a plan?"

"Not really." Ellie's mate sighed. "I've cooled off from when your dad told his story, but dammit, I'm not backing down. I've seen the sign."

Ellie looked at him. "What sign?"

Caleb drew down his brows and shifted in his seat. "I've been waiting for a sign to know when the time was right to fight Rocco. I got that sign, from my dad, no less. So this is it, no matter what."

"But your dad has been gone a long time. How..." She didn't know how to finish her sentence without sounding condescending.

"You held the other half of the sign, Ells." He smiled at her and squeezed her hand. "I've heard the words 'Castor oil' twice in my life. Once from you and once from my father. That's all I need to believe."

Ellie thought he was sort of reaching with that combination, but if that was what he believed, then she'd believe, too. "Okay, babe. Let's do this."

The alpha house came into sight. A few gasps escaped the men in the truck. "Caleb, what the hell has happened to the place? It looks almost condemned." Paint peeled, gutters hung down in a couple places. The grass was a foot high with weeds choking the once colorful flower beds. A broken window on the second floor was held together with duct tape.

"It goes with the owner. Should be torn down and burned in hell." Caleb sounded as if in his own world. Ellie wondered if something happened to her mate in the house. His look of disgust was too deep.

Several cars were parked along the circular drive. Caleb slowed while still on the street. Ellie studied him. She saw a touch of fear in him, but anger overrode his smell. Her mate was going in strong. Caleb leaned forward and reached his hand under the seat, coming up with a pistol in hand. Ellie sucked in a sharp breath.

Caleb tucked the weapon behind his back, under his shirt. "Don't worry, my love. It's only if things get out of hand. I don't trust my uncle one inch. And since I know you ladies won't stay in the truck, I have to be ready for anything."

Ellie gave him a serious nod and swallowed hard. "You're right about that. I'm no longer staying out of the picture while this crazy bastard does what he wants. We're a team and we will act like one. You got that, Your Behind-ness?" She smiled at Emma's silly word, hoping to lighten the tension.

Caleb parked along the side of the driveway, allowing for easy escape, if needed. She was going to suggest that if he hadn't already done it. Her confidence in her mate soared. She loved him and would battle alongside him.

Everyone piled out of the vehicle, staring at the dilapidated home.

CHAPTER Twenty Two

CALEB PARKED THE truck in the driveway positioned for a quick getaway, if needed. He didn't think his uncle would do anything drastic since this was a surprise visit, but he wanted to be prepared. His mate and the other mates were here and he would protect them with his life.

When seeing the cars lining in the drive, he had slowed their approach. That night, so long ago, when Rocco wanted to 'make a man' out of Caleb, rocketed through his head. What would he and the group find when they walked into the house? An orgy full on? During a Sunday afternoon? If that wasn't reason enough for a lightning bolt to strike his uncle, he didn't know what was.

Whatever was going on in the house would soon be public knowledge.

Caleb knocked on the front door instead of barging in. He could at least give the women time to cover themselves, if they cared. A strung-out blonde finally opened the door. "What do you want?" She squinted her eyes from the sun.

Caleb studied her, trying to remember if he knew her. "Who are you?"

She snorted. White powder flew from her nose. She giggled. "Oops, busted." She turned and walked away, leaving the door open. Caleb listened for telltale signs of the goings-on as he pushed the door open wider and stepped inside. All seemed quiet. Not even a TV was on.

The others followed behind as silently as the house was. The mates mumbled to each other as they progressed to the front room. Shambles was a nice way to describe the interior's condition. The odor of body sweat and sex permeated the air.

Caleb heard Aric telling Jordan, "Don't touch or sit on anything and leave your shoes on. No telling what you could be stepping on. Especially if squishy." A couple *ewwws* came from the girls. Aric was probably joking, but Caleb knew he was right.

Several scantily clad women and a couple younger guys were draped over furniture in the large living area. Mirrors and razor blades and plastic bags of white powder covered the coffee table between all the sofas.

Ellie grabbed his arm. "Caleb, you told me you didn't ever want to live in the alpha house again, but you never let on it was this bad. Oh my god, what does the pack think of this?"

He shrugged. "From those I talk to, I hear they hate it. But if they react, Rocco finds a way to retaliate. Like giving daughters to his enforcers for 'dates.'" That thought brought back his anger and vengeance for his people.

Rocco wasn't in the living room, but Caleb smelled his scent, along with several others from his pack, all familiar. He followed it down the hall to the den's closed doors. This time, he didn't bother knocking. He threw the doors open and walked in.

"Good afternoon, Uncle." Caleb scanned the room. Around a dozen of the larger men in the pack and Rocco's enforcers sat or stood, all facing his uncle sitting behind his platform-raised desk. He looked to be seated on a throne with his peons gathered to him. Caleb wanted to vomit.

Rocco's expression of surprise pleased Caleb. Perhaps for once, the underdog would have the upper hand. But he wouldn't remain suppressed much longer. "Aren't you happy to see me?"

Caleb almost sneered but remembered others were in the room. He would remain respectful as long as he could.

Rocco's eyes narrowed as the group walked into the dark room. "Of course I'm glad to see my nephew. It's been quite a while. To what do I owe this pleasure?"

Caleb stepped onto the raised stage and approached the massive cherry wood desk. One of the enforcers at his uncle's side stepped forward, but Rocco waved him off. Caleb, wearing an oversized, overdone smile, grabbed up his uncle's hand and shook it vigorously.

"And the pleasure is all yours, Uncle." He paused and looked each man in the room in the eye. He wanted to remember everyone here. A few he expected, a few were a surprise. "Did I interrupt a meeting?"

Rocco steepled his hands in front of his chin. "We were just having a social get-together to catch up on things." Several men in the crowd frowned, and Caleb caught angry glances come and go quickly.

"So I gather, Uncle." He plopped onto the corner of the desk to partially face both Rocco and the group. "My friends and I," he gestured to the Wolfe clan standing at the back of the room, "are here for the same reason. Sorta." Caleb turned feigned-happy eyes to the alpha. "We've discovered some things my pack would love to know."

Rocco flashed him a flinty stare. "Perhaps we should talk in private." He stood from his chair.

Caleb popped to his feet from the desk corner. "No, Rocco. I think they would want to hear this firsthand." All jovialness left his demeanor.

His uncle raised his hand and his enforcer stepped forward. "No, I'd rather—"

One of the pack men stood from his chair. "Yes, Alpha Rahound, we would like to hear." Several men nodded and mumbled agreement.

Rocco once again stopped his lackey, then smiled to Caleb. "Tell me, nephew, how is your dear mother doing? I'm sure the money I'm giving her pays for all her medical bills and medication." His uncle's smile turned devious but Caleb was ready for this manipulation; he'd done his homework. Rocco had used his mother as an unspoken bargaining chip for a long time.

"Yes, the money my father's life insurance provides does take care of the former true alpha's wife. I'm glad Dad set that up so only Mom and I can touch it. Otherwise it might have been spent a long time ago." Murmurs slid across the room. Who knew what Rocco told the pack about taking care of his mom. Probably that he was giving her money he shed sweat and tears for. Bastard.

Caleb continued. "And if you cared enough to check on her occasionally, you would know she's been out of the hospital for a while now." Rocco's face paled. He realized his biggest control factor over his nephew was gone. Caleb nodded to Aric and noted the Wolfe clan had spread out along the back of the room, making a loose, yet formidable, barrier. He owed his life to these people.

"With help from others, my mother has relocated to a secure place where I no longer have to worry about others using her for their own benefits." His look zeroed in on Rocco. Mumbles from the group again passed through the room.

Rocco stepped around to the front of his desk and glowered down at those sitting with rapt attention. "I've held you long enough. It's time you leave–"

Caleb pushed his uncle against the desk. "I'm not finished yet. I haven't mentioned the Wolfe's three babies you've kidnapped, or the people you've murdered, or the attempted murder on the Wolfe pack's alpha couple."

The crowd no longer remained quiet, including the enforcers. Pack members demanded to know what Caleb was talking about. Rocco's goons pushed and shoved members away from their alpha. Some threw fists, knocking over end tables and chairs. The aggression continued until Rocco and Caleb pulled guns on each other at the same time.

The audience silenced and the two stood face to face on the raised platform. Rocco smiled. "I see you've come prepared. Perhaps I've underestimated your resourcefulness."

"Damn right, you have," Caleb started. "You may have the rest of the pack controlled under fear of retribution, but you don't have me any longer. You've grown fat and lazy, Uncle. You assume I'm still the scared little boy running from your physical and mental abuse and rape attempts."

Caleb kept his uncle in the crosshairs of his Glock. He fought to keep the shame and fear of the past from engulfing him as it used to when he was younger. He was the victim, his people were still victims, but not for much longer. "Here's how this is going to play out, Uncle. I'm declaring a challenge for the right to be alpha of the Rahound pack. It will be a fight to the death. The pack members here have heard my announcement. Do you accept or step down?"

Rocco's face showed no emotion. "I accept your challenge to the death."

"Midnight tonight, be at the Scenting Field. It will be just you, me, and the council, Rocco. I will not let my pack suffer any longer under you and your sadistic tastes. You've tried to hurt others, and you've succeeded. But know if you harm one hair on the babies' heads, you will learn a new meaning to pain."

"I have no idea what you're talking about, nephew. Why would I want to hurt poor, helpless babies?" Rocco tried to sound innocent, but innocence was too far from his persona, he couldn't even fake it.

Caleb grunted. "For the same reason you cut the brake lines to cause the death of so many. Barbara Wolfe's brother, and Tristan and Barbara themselves, *my father*." Rocco laughed.

"Why would I want any of those wonderful people dead?"

"Nice try, Uncle. We all know the hierarchy to becoming an alpha. If one way didn't work, you found another that did." He waited for the others in the room to quiet. "Aric, you have anything you'd like to say before we call this meeting?" Glancing toward the Wolfe group, he noticed that each brother had a gun pulled also. That was surprising. Guess they knew Rocco as well as he did.

"Yeah," Aric began. "Rocco, to make it official, as the current active alpha for the Wolfe Pack of Blue Creek, I'm declaring a challenge for the right to be alpha to the Rahound pack in retribution of the kidnapping and attempted murder of my family members. It will be a fight to the death. No one gets away with hurting my family or my pack. If Caleb doesn't take you down, I will. Do you accept or step down?"

Rocco's face turned dark red and his hands holding his gun

shook. "I accept the challenge to your death, Wolfe bastard. I will shred you alive. I hope your niece and nephews are safe while you fight me."

"You son of a bitch!" Before anyone realized what was happening, Karla sprang toward Rocco. Midair, her wolf exploded out, sending clothes shrapnel in all directions.

Nathan lunged after her. "Karla, no!"

Rocco didn't have time to react, but an enforcer stepped in front of his alpha and took the hit from the furious momma wolf. The two rolled and the wolf came up on top, human throat in her mouth. Caleb stepped closer to his uncle, putting his gun in his face to keep him or anyone else from shooting the wolf.

"Karla, stop." Nathan was instantly at his mate's side, talking her down from the blood lust she craved from threatening her children.

"You're lucky to be alive, Uncle. You should know better than to piss off a mother wolf. I'm done here. You have the challenge and six hours to prepare. Now, let the pack members in this room leave without threats of any kind. Then my friends and I will leave. Put down your gun and so will I."

Rocco had to know he stood no chance of surviving a shoot-out in the den. None of them would, probably. As his uncle brought his weapon down, so did Caleb.

"I'll see you in several hours, Uncle. Have a great day."

CHAPTER Twenty Three

OPERATION SHITTY NO More had begun.

Raymond was the man for this mission. He looked down at the two babies lying quietly on the bathroom floor, intensely staring at him. Damn that freaked him out. It's like they knew what was going on and would zap him with lightning bolts from their eyes if he messed up. He shook it off. He had to focus.

Dressed in a full apron, backward baseball cap, clothespin on his nose, and yellow latex gloves securely fastened, Ray approached the tub holding the enemy within. The tiny face giggled and gurgled at him, waving arms and legs. He focused on the bottom half of the body—the enemy's stronghold.

Open trash bag in hand, he knelt and bent over the tub's edge. The clothespin pushed up, snapped together, and fell, leaving him defenseless to the smell. He quickly snatched it back up and stuck it on, clipping his nostrils closed.

He studied the diaper fit snuggly under a bulging baby belly. Two strips across the top front looked like a good means to access the enemy. Ray's gloved hands reached down and pulled the strips to the side. They easily pulled away and lay against the tub's bottom.

The critical moment was just ahead. The success or failure of Operation Shitty No More depended on his next move. Slowly, carefully, he lifted the front section of the diaper and pulled it away.

He saw the enemy. Ewww. Shit. Shit was the enemy. *Don't throw up. Don't throw up.* Seconds mattered. *Don't throw up.* He pulled the diaper up (*don't throw up*) and into the trash bag with one sweeping motion. He quickly tied a knot in the bag and tossed it into the hallway. Enemy camp destroyed. Mission complete.

The first part of the operation had been a success. But the enemy clung to the baby's skin. Ewww. *Don't throw up.*

Ray shed the thick yellow gloves and turned the tub handles to get the right temperature of water. Removing the handheld nozzle for the showerhead, he pushed the knob to redirect the water flow from faucet to hose. A soft rain pattered over the tub's drain. He aimed the hose toward the naked baby now giggling harder. It seemed the warm droplets tickled. The two others on the floor laughed probably because the infected body in the tub did.

After the enemy was washed away, he put the handheld head into its holder. Then, lifting the happy ex-hostage over the tub, Ray turned the baby, making sure of complete shit removal. He placed the saved child on the towel on the floor and dried him off. Now came the scariest and most difficult part of Operation Shitty No More: putting on a clean diaper, for all three.

Free to remove the clothespin, he kept the backward cap and apron on for security reasons. The enemy could sneak out at any time during this deployment. He laid Baby One on the bed, then retrieved Boy Two and the girl. All three, once again, stared up at him, happy little grins shining.

He was suddenly nervous. He'd seen those grins before, just before Baby One burped from the wrong end. He had to be fast. He looked at the bedside table and the containers on it. Tonya's list said diaper stuff was in the bedroom.

There were wipes, white creams, powders, moisturizer, ointments, petroleum jelly, cotton balls, Q-Tips, toys, and binkies. *What the fuck?* Was he supposed to use all this?

Okay, he got what the baby wipes were for, but the Q-Tips? Was he really supposed to clean inside *that* area? He'd leave that for when Tonya got back. No way was he doing any cleaning of the kind.

Baby One already had a shower, so he was clean. Enough. Ray pulled out a diaper and he laid it next to the boy. Shit, the diaper's top was at the babe's chin. He looked at the pack to see what size they were. Nobody told Tonya how old the babies were so she purchased a case of multi-sized diapers. Great.

He put the current diaper to the side as too big, for now. Fishing around in the plastic surrounding the sizes, he pulled out the smallest one. It looked right.

He stuck half of the open diaper under the baby's bottom and folded the top half up. He searched for the tab of tape that held the front and back together. He finally found it on the inside of the top half. What a stupid place for that to be. It was hard to get to. He pulled the tab covering off and had to pull more diaper to the side to get the tab to reach the back half.

When he went to do the other side, he found there was no way the tab would reach the back piece. There were about four inches of tummy between taper and tapee. Well, shit. This one was too small. It sure looked like it would fit. In taking the diaper off, he had to pull and tear the strong plastic the tab was stuck to. He didn't remember having to do that in the bathtub. That would've been an enemy disaster.

Next he pulled out a size between the two already tried. This time went much quicker because he knew the tabs were on the top piece's backside. Still he had trouble getting the tape to sit right. After the diaper was attached, Ray lifted the baby to take pride in his first-ever baby change.

It looked a little strange. Sagged a bit. The material narrowed at the backside and gapped. Maybe these diapers didn't have the same coverage area as the previous ones. But it sure needed to be wider in the back—wait a minute. He glanced at the diaper Boy Two had on. The tape tabs were on the opposite side. He put the damn thing on backwards. Shit.

He ripped at the tape, again stuck to the stretchy plastic. What a dumb idea. They needed a piece of slick paper to attach the tab to; this tearing was ridiculous.

The third attempt was successful. And they did have a plastic tab to attach the tape to. Plus the tape was much easier to find this time. It was on the *back* piece. Who knew? Yes, Baby One was a success.

Since the girl was laying quieter than the boy in the middle, he'd take care of her next. After removing the old diaper, he had to get the trash with the enemy in it to put this one with it. He held his breath when opening the bag but kept his eyes open. He saw the enemy. *Don't throw up.*

Bag retied, he plucked the same size diaper from the case and quickly whipped it on the girl. He lifted her and the diaper slid down her legs and hung onto one foot, swinging. She smiled and made a noise, slapping her arms up and down. *What the fuck?* Comparing her to the first baby, she was much smaller than he was. Shit.

He laid her down and reached into the bag for the smallest size again. Finally, second baby finished.

He tried to slide the diaper that fell off the girl onto the middle boy, but the waist was taped to tightly. Should've known when he had to wrap the tape around to the back of the diaper that it was too big for her. Live and learn.

But at least he knew the diaper size for the boy was right. Ray discarded the old diaper and as he bent to slide the diaper under the last tiny butt, warm liquid shot up and hit him in the face. *What the fuck?* The kid peed on him. Shit.

He raced to the bathroom and scrubbed his face with soap and water. *Don't throw up.* Fuck, this was gross. How did women do this stuff all day long? He returned fresh and clean to the three babies wiggling around on the bed. Thank god they couldn't crawl. That would've been a disaster.

Ray finished up the third diaper but didn't lift him. He didn't want to know if it fit or not. He had an idea to ensure the size worked.

Thirty minutes, six diapers, and three yards of duct tape wrapped around three small waists later, Operation Shitty No More was completed.

Ray lay on the bed next to the babies. He was pooped. No pun intended. This was just too much for him. He took a deep breath and quickly dozed off.

CHAPTER Twenty Four

ELLIE SAT IN front of the computer in her father's office keying an email to the entire pack about the challenge in a few hours. Her brothers were calling everyone they could to join in the fight. She hoped many would show their solidarity and pride for the pack and its leaders.

She realized this was practice for her responsibilities to come. Nerves were getting the best of her. What if she wasn't good enough to handle the position? What if everyone hated her because she was from the enemy's side?

Caleb's calming scent surrounded her. She breathed deeply as soft lips touched her neck. "What's wrong, sweetheart? Are you worried about the fight?"

"It's nothing."

"I believe I've learned that *nothing* means something, and I need to found out right now what that is."

Ellie smiled, remembering the earlier conversation. It felt like days ago, but it had only been hours. "Hold on a sec." She wrapped up her email and clicked send.

Caleb took her hand. "Let's go outside for a minute." Ellie smiled wider remembering what happened the last time they went outside for a talk. Not a whole lot of talking.

Her mate guided her to the picnic table on the shaded side of the house, opposite of where those inside were. He straddled the bench seat and pulled her to sit in front of him. His hands squeezed her shoulders. "You're too stressed, sweetheart. Let me relax you."

Ellie laughed. "Translated to you want to cop a feel."

"Maybe." Ellie heard the smile in his voice. "With your permission, of course." His massaging hands rubbed her upper back.

"God, that feels so good."

Caleb kissed the side of her neck. "I know what else that will make you feel good."

"You do, do you?" Her grin grew, heat starting in her lower stomach.

His thumbs circled between her shoulder blades while his fingers slid sideways, brushing her breasts. Slowly, his fingers glided to her nipples, teasing and pinching them taut. God, he knew just how to touch her. Every time.

Ellie sighed and leaned into his hot body, letting his lips skate down her neck and the top of her shoulder. Each nip of his fingers on her breasts sent a line of fire straight to her pussy. Her heat quickly built, releasing her mind from the stress of reality. This was what she needed. His touch. Something only he could give her. Her mate.

Rough fingertips slipped under her shirt and skipped over her skin, then pushed her breast up and out of her bra cup. The flesh-on-flesh tingled to her clit. Oh, good god!

His other hand slid beneath her waistband, seeking her swelling button. The pad of a finger stopped on her clit and rubbed small circles. *Fuck.* It felt so good. His hand dipped to her core, spooned out her wetness, then returned, leaving a slick trail up her pussy lips. Her belly fluttered and need spread through her like hot lava.

With a twist of her nipple and squeeze to her tight button, Ellie arched her torso and came hard. Her mate kept up the delicious torture as she rode the wave. A finger fell to her core, sneaking in and out in perfect rhythm to her orgasmic spikes.

"Fuck, Ellie. I need inside you." He unbuttoned her slacks, then unsnapped his pants and slid them low enough for his hard cock to stand proudly.

"Caleb," she started hoarsely but stopped. What could she say? She wanted him inside her, too. "Hurry up."

He was beautiful. Every time she saw him even a little naked, her heart tripped. He leaned her forward, still straddling the bench seat, and slipped her pants down as far as they would go. She clung to him for support.

He lifted her ass off the bench and buried his cock in her dripping core.

"Ah, baby. This will never get old," he grunted, pressing his pelvis flush to hers.

She gasped with the sudden fullness, loving the sensation. This. He knew exactly what she needed.

"Do you feel that, sweetheart?" he groaned, his cock gripped tightly by her pussy. "Your tension melted the moment my dick was inside you."

She cleared her throat. "So you're saying you have a magic cock?"

He chuckled roughly by her ear. "No, baby girl. What I have is the touch you need." His hands found their way under her shirt and around her breasts, pulling and tweaking the nipples. He slammed in and out of her pussy. "Now," he snarled, fucking her to the point she could barely breathe, "I just need to make sure your pussy's squeezing my cum soon."

Ellie met his every thrust, driving herself higher and higher. "Squeeze me, Ellie. Tighten around my cock." She focused on her Kegel muscles, clasping them. "That's it, baby. Fuck, that feels great. Tighter." Her face scrunched with effort. "Get your hot little pussy sucking my cock tight!" She gritted her teeth, trying to crush them together. His pounding increased. "More." The growl in his voice and the effect of her Kegels sent her exploding into orgasm.

She rent her scream into her sleeve to not draw attention. Caleb lifted from the bench, arching as he came.

Breathing heavily, she sat back, his cock still pulsing inside her. His chest heaved against her. "Damn, sweetheart. You sure know how to relax."

EMMA FROWNED AT the computer screen. The stupid search results were not telling her what she needed to know. Were she and Mason officially married? Maybe she could find someone to marry them tonight or early tomorrow morning, just to make sure.

Being Sunday, all the government offices were closed, so finding another justice of the peace wouldn't do any good. She was sure none of the local religious ministers would marry them on the spot. She'd have to go another route. Weren't boat captains able to marry people? She googled for area captains.

The only site she found that said the captain worked on Sunday was Bubba's Shrimp Boats and More. She was not getting married on a shrimp boat. She didn't even know such boats were around there. Shrimp certainly weren't.

Emma wracked her brain for possible others who could marry them. There were Native Americans nearby. She wondered if a Shaman would marry them. Then she remembered a story she read where the bride and groom had to sit in a sweat lodge for hours. That would ruin her hair and makeup for pictures. That wasn't an option. *Shit.* This was looking hopeless.

Mason came up behind her and kissed the top of her head. "Whacha doing, sweetheart?"

Emma let out a deep sigh and said nothing. Mason stiffened around her then pulled away, headed for the door. She twisted in her chair to look at him. "Where are you going?"

His eyes were wide with worry. "It'll be okay, babe. I will get you sweets and make some spaghetti and you'll be happy again."

What was he talking about? "Mason," she stood, "I don't want spaghetti. I need you." She couldn't help the tears stinging her eyes. If she lost Mason because of some dead person's administrative fuck-up, she wouldn't be able to cope.

He swept her into his arms. "What's wrong, sweetheart? And don't say nothing, because I forgot what do for that."

She didn't care what his crazy talk was about as long as he was with her. "I'm worried about the Central pack taking you away from me. I will kill them before that happens. I can't, won't, live without you. Not after all the shit we've been through. And don't you even suggest that I be your mistress. You'll die first."

He chuckled and kissed her pout. "Sweetheart, I would never suggest that. You are my heart, my mate, and we are married whether paperwork is filed or not. Either we both go to the Central pack as a couple or we don't go at all." He lifted her chin and laid a soulful, hot kiss on her.

Mason rubbed his hardened cock against her soft flesh and they came up for air. He said, "Just to be on the safe side, can't ship captains marry people?"

Emma scowled, ready to pommel him.

He laughed. "I'm kidding, brat." She punched him in the stomach for good measure.

CHAPTER
Twenty Five

RAYMOND'S SEXY HOT girlfriend straddled him on the bed and kissed him. She worked her sweet tongue along his jaw to his ear. She stuck a sloppy lick over his ear canal then bit down on his lobe, causing a bit of pain.

"Hey, baby. I know you like it rough and raw, but dial back on the teeth there. Just tongue me, baby."

Her hot hand slid across his forehead then back over his head. Wet kisses returned to his lips at the same time another bite stung his ear.

"Babe—" her tongue dipped into his open mouth and snapped out like a tease. Again, and once again. Her nails scratched down the side of his face and his ear stabbed with pain. Ray was losing patience. "Okay, woman."

His girlfriend looked at him and yipped. *What the hell?* She licked his nose and gave a tiny bark. Her breath smelled like a dog's.

Ray's eyes opened to see a tiny snout and blue eyes staring at him. The little pup licked his nose again and sat on his throat, her tongue lolling to the side. Next to his ear, another furball growled and yanked his lobe with sharp canines. Tugging and twisting in his hair told him where the third pup played.

"What the hell? Y'all can't transform yet. You're too young. Even I know that." He thought about his dream with his girlfriend French kissing him, then eyed the pup's tongue lolling out. He jumped off the bed and ran for the door. Ray ran the opposite direction of the miscreants. He had to scrape his tongue and brush his teeth, at least twice.

This was so not his gig. He had nothing against rugrats and ankle biters, except they were a pain in his ass. A loud crash came from the other room and Ray was on his feet instantly. He hurried down the hall. "Hey, whatever you're doing, cut it out. I ain't cleaning no messes around here."

He stopped in the entrance to the kitchen. Ray noted one of the furry behinds had a diaper on with duct tape still around the waist. That little one sat on top of the refrigerator next to a cookie jar and stared down at the open fridge door below him. Shit.

Ray glanced lower to see a pair of hind legs and wagging tail sticking out between the fridge door and its frame. How the furry little monster got the door open was beyond him. The tail disappeared and the door closed. Shit.

Ray hurried to get the crotch fruit out of potential danger. He pulled the door open and bent down to find the kid. He heard a scraping sound above, and then felt a heavy pain shoot through his head and knock him to the floor. For fuck's sake!

Laying on his back, he gazed up to see the pup wearing a diaper with his head dangling over the front side of the fridge, tongue hanging. Ray rolled his head to the side to see the ceramic cookie jar in pieces. The little shit pushed it off the top onto his head. Who did this wise, diaper-wearing ass think he was?

A muffled bark came from inside the fridge. The biggest of the twat goblins scurried to the fridge. He lay on his back and put his paws under the door and pushed until the door opened. The one inside was leaning on the door also, and when it swung opened, jumped from a wire rack with a Ziploc back of fried chicken in her mouth. Shit.

On the way to the floor, the package wedged between two bottles of salad dressing in the door shelf. Her teeth held onto the plastic as she dangled. Her body weight stretched the bag until it tore and chicken splatted on the floor. Dinner was served.

Still laying on the floor, Ray rose to his elbows to stare at the mess. A sudden sharp pain shot from his groin to his stomach. The crib-midget on top of the refrigerator had jumped, landing on his balls, then scurried to the food the other two partook.

Ray curled into a ball on his side and growled through his teeth. The littlest ankle biter looked at him and cocked her head. She sank her teeth into a fried drumstick, dragged it toward Ray, and set it in front of his face. She then scooted it against his mouth with her head. The little princess sat and peered at him for a few seconds, then she leaned forward, licked his eye, and frolicked back to her brothers.

The smart pup with the diaper jumped onto the cabinet and bumped his head against the sink faucet handle, making the water run. He lapped at the flow as the other two joined him. They pushed each other and splashed around, creating a mess. Ray climbed to his feet to put a stop to it.

The largest of the cute demons fell against the backsplash and wedged himself between the wall and separate handheld sink sprayer. His big belly pushed against the sprayer, streaming water in an elegant fall over the basin to the floor. Shit, now there was water everywhere for Ray to clean. Shit.

Ray reached for one of the wet rats as she twisted her body to shake off the water on her coat. He squeezed his eyes closed and turned his head away. When he looked back, all three were disappearing down the hallway. Shit.

Ray turned the water off and went after them. He wondered how the babies morphed into their wolf souls so quickly. Science speculated that nature suppressed the instinct until babies were old enough to comprehend the alter self. Maybe the little mutants were older than Rahound told him.

He stepped into the living room. Mid-stride, a blur ran past his feet. He tried not to step on it and stumbled to his knees on the hard tile floor. Shit, that hurt. A growl reached his ears and he turned to see white fluff in the air floating to the floor. One of the semen demons whipped a small sofa pillow around in its teeth, gnashing and growling. The material was torn, shooting stuffing into the air with each thrash of the pillow.

Ray sighed and crawled toward the sofa. His hand came down on something squishy and he saw the used rubber he flung from the couch earlier. His arm flew up, shifting his balance sideways and he hit his head against the coffee table. Fluff rained over his face causing him to sneeze.

Two of the crotch fruit chased each other. Ray's stomach happened to be in their path. The diaper devil jumped over him, but the bigger bastard launched too early and landed its back end on Ray's solar plexus. Air whooshed from his lungs.

He rolled over to catch his breath, his nose brushing against the rubber condom. His head shot back as the two boys ran over his skull, one getting its belly stuck on his ear, legs too short to continue. Ray jumped to his feet, face in a snarl. "Okay, enough of this shit. Everyone settle down."

The three tiny hoodlums stopped and looked innocently at him. Yeah, right. He wasn't that much of a sucker.

Standing, looking as angelic as possible, one lifted his leg next to a plant. Ray dove for the twat droppling. "Oh, no you don't." The little one barked, laughing puppy style, and zoomed away. Ray chased the pee-er around the coffee table. He reached down to scoop it up and slammed his jaw on the dark wooden top. Unfortunately, his tongue happened to be between his front teeth at that time.

He fell into a chair in front of the window and howled with pain, a coppery taste coating his mouth. A big ripping sound came behind him and he looked over his shoulder to see front paws with claws out sliding down the curtain panel. That side of the metal curtain rod snapped and hurtled toward his face. Shit.

His eyes rotated toward the other side of the room, where Diaper Butt had batted off the lid to the aquarium and proceeded to fall into the tank reaching for an angelfish. Shit, shit.

The third sniffed around a plant again. Real shit.

Chapter Twenty Six

MIDNIGHT AT THE field of good and evil. Caleb snorted as he stood beside Ellie along the edge of the Scenting field. Evil didn't begin to describe his asshole uncle.

The cool air was as still as the creatures of the forest. The proverbial quiet before the storm. And what a storm was in store for this field. Last he was here, Marco and Kelly were taking the first steps to starting a new life together. Now, he was here to end one.

Ellie squeezed his hand. She was beside him and he felt empowered. He was stupid to think he was protecting her by not letting her help him in the battle against Rocco. She had been attacked multiple times by rogue wolves. Encouraging her to train in self-defense with Mike was one of the smartest decisions he'd ever made. Or had Ellie made that choice on her own?

Didn't matter. What did was what he had learned by keeping her away: without his partner by his side, he would never be complete. There would always be something missing from him. They were born to be together, born to guide and love their people as true leaders should.

They would turn the Rahound pack around. Together, they could heal the damage done to the members and gradually bring back those who escaped to other packs. He had a great mentor to help him along. Ellie's dad, Tristan, was the perfect example of a husband, father, and alpha.

Caleb wished his father was still alive to offer advice. He wondered how everything would be if his father hadn't died in the wreck. Tristan and Barbara lived, why couldn't his father have? He was a strong alpha. All he had to do was shift once to heal enough to live.

Caleb shook his head to clear those thoughts from his mind. He loved Ellie, her parents and her brothers, even though they were sometimes overprotective of their little sister. But that was okay. He was, too.

On the other side of the clearing, Rocco and a few of his enforcers walked out of the dense woods. Behind them were a handful of men and women—the Rahound council. The council took their place in the center of the field between the two groups.

The time had come.

Caleb said, "I was beginning to wonder if you'd show, Uncle."

Rocco's sneer was evident even at this distance. "Don't be so eager to die, boy."

Ellie squeezed his hand again and he smelled her fear. He took her into his arms and kissed her. "Don't worry, sweetheart. I fight with you in my soul which gives me the strength to overpower anyone. Except your dad, maybe."

Rocco grunted. "Such sweet words, Romeo. Now get out here so we can get this over with. I got shit to do, women to fuck."

Caleb turned toward the field and gave a quick nod. "Let it begin, Uncle. *According to tradition.*"

"Figured you'd say that." With evident disgust, Rocco brushed his hand through the air at the council. "Get it going."

One of the men ceremoniously unrolled a scroll and read: "A challenge to the death for the alpha position of the Rahound Pack has been made by Caleb Rahound, son of Conly Rahound, former alpha, and accepted by interim alpha, Rocco Rahound, brother of previous alpha. Alpha Rahound, do you bring witnesses who will acclaim your worthiness?"

Behind Rocco, people poured out from the forest. Men and a few women from the Rahound pack, tough looking strangers Caleb knew to be rogues, others he didn't know, and several vampires, including a dapper dark-haired gentlemen dressed in genuine dojo attire.

"Fuck," a surprised and shocked Ellie and Caleb said at the same time. An alpha challenge needed only a few to verify tradition was followed. What did Rocco have planned with so many followers?

Rocco looked more than smugly pleased. "I bring witnesses who will acclaim my worthiness." He gestured to his group. "As you see, I'm well admired."

The council turned to his side. "Caleb Rahound, do you bring witnesses who will acclaim your worthiness?"

Behind him and Ellie, people stepped forward from the trees. In the lead were her brothers and their mates, Jaxon and his men followed. Trevan and his guys headed out with Aria and her three powerhouses. Behind them, it looked like the entire Wolfe pack had come.

To Caleb's surprise, several pack members on Rocco's side ran across the field to join their enemy. Their action further solidified in Caleb's mind what he was doing was the right thing for his pack.

Rocco's smile quickly faded. Caleb grinned. "I bring witnesses who will acclaim my worthiness." He let his quantity of supporters speak for themselves toward his admiration.

"Challengers come forward and stand in front of me." Both men stepped toward the center of the field, each eyeing up the other's potential. The elite member continued. "The rule for the challenge is simple: if a challenger leaves the fighting circle for any reason, they forfeit."

The councilman looked up from the paper. "The circle is a twenty-five feet radius from this point where we stand." Caleb noted the distance stopped where the grass ended and the gravel parking area started. He'd have to get Rocco to the sidelines or onto the rocky parking lot. "Do you understand the rule as given?"

Both challengers said yes.

The council hurried to the top of the circle and stood just beyond the grass. One of the ladies raised her hand. "Let the challenge begin." Her arm dropped to her side.

The two combatants circled each other. "So, son–"

"Don't call me son. There would be nothing more despising than being your offspring. Good thing your line officially stops here."

Red reflected in Rocco's eyes a second before his transformation. Rocco's wolf leapt at Caleb's head, claws spread to rip out a huge chunk of flesh. But his target vanished and he arched as he felt a pain in his chest. Caleb had morphed into his wolf and remained underneath, claws held up to drag the vulnerable belly. Rocco's twist upward saved his life.

Two wolves circled each other, each waiting for the opportunity to attack. Rocco swiped a paw over Caleb's muzzle, leaving a few bleeding scratches. Rocco laughed at his cheap shot but even something so innocuous wore down the fighter.

After waiting for so long for Rocco to play his trick, Caleb attacked. He was tired of waiting for the coward. Fur flew, teeth flashed, red claws raised and slashed through the air. The battle became a blur in motion.

Groups on both sides cheered their contestant, offering advice and useless help.

The wolves broke apart, panting, circling. Rocco pushed for a telepathic connection which Caleb accepted. "Well, boy, you're holding your end so far. How long can you last against a real alpha?"

"Uncle, I'll let you know when I fight one."

Rocco snapped his teeth at Caleb. He dodged the second cheap shot. "You little shit, you've always been a pain in my ass." A feeling of smugness passed through the link. "Tell me, pansy ass, are you still a virgin? What *man* runs from a group of women who want to fuck? I was so disappointed in you. But you're your father's son. Pathetic."

Caleb refused the bait his uncle dangled. A cool mind prevailed in the end. "What's the plan, Uncle?"

"Ah, yes. You'd like to know that before you die. And I'm dying to tell you." Laughter carried between the connection, only from Rocco's side. "No pun intended, of course. My dear nephew, I intend to take your little girlfriend and treat her just as I would've her beautiful mother."

Caleb's heart stumbled. "You're thirty years older. She'll never agree, you overgrown piece of shit. You're disgusting."

"No, what's disgusting," Rocco began, "is all the delicious things I plan to do to her scrumptious body."

"You will never touch her!" Caleb cut the link between the two and lunged at his enemy.

Chapter Twenty Seven

PURE FURY ROLLED through Caleb. His mate had been threatened with the worst thing imaginable—mental and physical abuse. Not in this fucking lifetime. Caleb would die fighting for her.

Gashes flowed freely with his blood. Kudos to Rocco for keeping up his fighting skills, but Caleb was younger with more stamina, and more of a reason to win. He noted how close they were getting to the top of the perimeter. He didn't want Rocco taking a cheap shot to get him to step over the line.

With a quick twist move, Caleb had Rocco pinned to the ground, jaws clamped around the bastard's throat. Their mental tie opened. "Surrender, Rocco, or I will crush your neck. This fight is to the death, but I don't want to kill you and lose another family member. Step down from alpha and I will let you leave alive."

Again, laughter transferred from one to the other. "You're such a pussy. A coward, just like your father."

"Rocco, that was the dumbest thing you've ever sai–"

Caleb's wolf form flew back from his grounded opponent. A pain shot through his body that almost knocked him unconscious. The answer to his curious affliction came to him on the wind: the sound of a gunshot.

EVERYONE LOOKED AT the trees on the Rahound side of the field except Ellie. She darted toward Caleb who was lying on his side, panting. She slid to her knees, taking her mate's furry head into her lap.

"Oh my god, Caleb." Her hands raised, completely covered in blood. Ellie focused on Rocco. "You son of a bitch. You shot him. You cheated!"

The alpha of the Rahound pack returned to his human body. "*I didn't shoot him.* Now get out of the way so I can rip out his throat."

Adrenalin shot through Ellie's body. She couldn't allow this. "He's injured. You can't attack him."

Rocco's brow drew up. "The fight continues, my soon to be sex slave, until only one lives or he leaves the circle. You can drag him out, but he forfeits and you belong to me." His tongue slid between his lips. Caleb whined and moved in her lap.

She whispered to him, "No, Caleb. Do your best to heal yourself." Ellie laid his head on the ground and stood. "I invoke the universal rule to fight in place of my mate."

Caleb whined again and shouts came from the Wolfe side of the field, mainly from her brothers and their mates. She held up a hand to quiet them.

Rocco smiled. "Nice try, my pet, but you two are not fully mated."

Ellie smiled back. "We're legally married in the human world, which wolf law considers fully mated. And as the offended party, I choose we fight in human form." More angry shouts filled the air.

A scowl consumed her enemy's face. "Either way is fine with me. I think I'll take you down and fuck you right here for everyone to see our mating."

Ellie smiled. "Let's tango, shall we?" She stepped away from Caleb, to the middle of the fighting circle, and held her hand out to Rocco.

His head tilted. "What's this? You truly wish to tango, perhaps?" She remained quietly standing with a pleasant smile. As soon as he placed his hand in hers, she twirled into his arms, putting her back against his front. Ellie promptly stomped on his toes with the heel of her hiking boot, jabbed her elbow into his solar plexus, grabbed his arm around her, and flipped him over her back.

Rocco landed flat, face up, to laughter from both sides. Taunts of "you're letting a girl beat you" and "the girl's whipping your ass" enraged him. He sprang to his feet and came at her. Again, he ended up on his back. Mike's training was worth his weight in gold.

A phone ringing barely registered with her. Shortly thereafter, a hushed whisper spread through the group on her side. Whatever was going on, she'd find out later. Ellie flipped Rocco again.

This time she took him down, his face against the ground, her arm locked around his neck. She knew what he'd experience next. As she applied pressure, his vision would narrow on his way to unconsciousness. "Listen up, Rocco. I don't want to kill you. I'm not like the dirt you are. So you can walk away and forfeit right now, or I'll drag your knocked out ass over the line. Which is it?"

One of Ellie's brothers yelled from the Rahound side. "Hey, everyone. Look what I found." The crowd divided, allowing Aric to stride forward. He held a rifle in one hand with the other wrapped around a male's neck. "Seems this guy thinks it's hunting season. Since there is no hunting wolves, I'm not sure what he was aiming at."

Aric shook the man by the collar then looked at Rocco in Ellie's hold. "I'd ask you if you know this guy, but I see you're busy." He laughed and headed toward the other side of the field.

The dark-haired vampire stood with his hands on his hips on the sideline in front of Rocco. "If I'd known you were such a pantywaist, Rocco, I'd never have agreed to fight with you."

From the crowd came Aria's voice. "Filip, you truly are a piece of shit. This ends now." As Aria with Julian, Penelope, and Zane made their way through the crowd, Rocco took the distracted opportunity to shift to his animal. He whipped out of Ellie's hold and dove for her neck with his razor teeth flashing.

Ellie yelped and got her forearm up in time to keep the wolf's jaw from crunching her throat. He morphed into his human. "You're like your mate, too pussy to kill the enemy. I don't have that problem. Your pack will be mine like it should've been years ago before your father came along and took your mother from me."

Fire burned in her eyes. "My brothers won't let that happen."

"Then, my dearest, you will no longer be an aunt to three little shits under my control." He signaled to someone on his sideline.

Chapter Twenty Eight

RAYMOND LAY ON the tile floor, eyes staring blankly at the ceiling in the destroyed living room, blood from his curtain-rod smashed nose seeping onto the front of his chest. His shirt still had wet devil spawn puke down the back.

The ground was littered with white and cream packing from different pillows. He thought maybe a half-chewed sofa cushion contributed also. The front curtains hung halfway off the brackets. One side was still attached, but the screw holding up the bar had slid partially out of the drywall.

His hands found their way into his own hair and was yanking and pulling. Maybe self-flagellation would save him from insanity.

It wasn't looking good.

He smelled fresh dirt, meaning one of the plants was a goner. At least he didn't have to change shitty diapers again. That seemed like days ago, but could only have been hours, right? Maybe this was all a dream. A nightmare his girlfriend inflicted on him because he didn't want to start a family yet. Now, it will be never. He giggled. Never!

He barely felt the sharp little teeth biting into his shoe. The sperm vermin would have the leather eaten in no time. Another of the crotch nuggets simply made laps around and around and around…her barking and howling getting louder with every round. A rough tongue licked a sore spot on his cheek.

Another giggle escaped his throat. This one dark and creepy. He freaked himself out hearing it. Rahound could babysit the frakenspawn if he wanted them. Would he snap soon?

Warm wetness spread along his ankle. He rolled his head to see a short furry leg lifted over his shoe. A creek of yellow liquid flowed over the strings.

RAY STARED OUT the windshield of his truck as a crib lizard chewed and tore open the passenger side seat cover. He didn't care. He barely noticed. The only thing running through his mind was no more babies, no more floor monsters, no more.

His truck turned onto the same driveway it had fifteen or sixteen hours—maybe days—ago. He wasn't keeping track of anything except no more babies, no more muff monkeys. He'd never felt so happy in his life as to get rid of the aliens that invaded his life. He should think about locating the mothership. He wouldn't want more Martians finding him. He giggled as he put the vehicle in park.

He knocked on a familiar front door, chanting his mantra: No more hellions…

A surprised young woman, the mother, answered the door. Before she had a chance to speak, Ray shoved three wide-eyed, tongue-lolling pups into her arms, one soaking wet with a drooping diaper. "No more babies." He giggled and stepped away. "No more babies." Taking a side step, he slammed into the house siding, bouncing off with a smile still on his face.

"No more babies!" He tripped down the steps to the front porch, "No more babies!" then stumbled to his truck, "No more babies," and slammed his head against the window, knocking himself out cold.

CHAPTER Twenty Nine

CALEB LAY BLEEDING in his wolf body, listening as Ellie invoked her right to fight in place of him, her mate. What the fuck was she thinking? After he saw her lay Rocco flat on his ass, he closed his wolf eyes and focused on healing the gunshot to his shoulder.

A phone ringing caught his attention and whispers floated. He saw Nate run to his brothers. He wondered what that was about. If it was another trick from Rocco, Caleb would saw off his uncle's balls with an emery board.

A pissed-off voice called out to someone named Filip.

Caleb's wolf eyes opened to see Rocco shift and attack Ellie, his teeth shredding her arm on his way to her throat. Her brothers launched into the fighting circle, but they were too far away to get to her before Rocco killed her.

Before his brain could register his reaction, he'd mowed over his uncle, dragging him away from his mate. All hell broke loose around them.

When the brothers and Aria stormed onto the field, Rahound's side took that to be a free for all. The two groups converged.

ARIA SAW FEAR cross Filip's face, until more vampires stepped to his side. Her focus zoomed in on the gorgeous vamp. "I don't care how you escaped the fire, cockhead. But now, I will end you."

Filip straightened and tugged on his pristine white Japanese fighting top. "Why won't you just go away? I'm so tired of dealing."

"Well, excuse the fuck out of me, asswipe." She swiped a clawed hand across his face. "Let me take care of your problem by killing you."

Filip's eyes twinkled black and he threw himself at her, mouth gaping, teeth ready to chomp. Aria met him head on, swinging an upper cut and snapping his head back hard enough to flip his body over.

From his prone position on the ground, Filip dove for her legs, taking her to the ground.

Aria rolled with her enemy, coming up straddling him. He bucked his hips, tossing her off. "I'd love to try that move naked with my dick buried inside you. I'd buck until you screamed my name, then drain you as you came around my cock."

A shudder passed through Aria. "Sounds disgusting, Filip. No wonder you're single. Females with any taste can't stand to be in your presence."

He grinned a sneer. "I assure you, women won't be standing while in my presence, but I do care for their taste as it flows over my tongue. My vampires will bleed out every one of you until no trace of the Valderi family exists."

Aria gave a little giggle. "You think a handful of vamps here could take out the strongest and oldest vampires in the world?"

"I will take you down on my own," Filip bragged. "My southern empire will do the rest. These men owe Rocco a debt. They are here to make good on it. And get a little wolf blood on the side." The vamps behind him snickered.

An *empire*? Aria didn't like the sound of that. After she killed Filip, she'd need to check out what was going on in the South. "I'm sure your empire is the size of your dick. Miniscule." The men behind Filip tittered, enraging him more. He came at her with a frontal assault.

She positioned herself as she did for the upper cut earlier. Filip adjusted to defend and throw his own punch. Aria squatted under his swing and crashed her head into his groin, her nails dragged down his thighs, digging deeply. He fell to the side, curled in a half ball. His pristine whites were not so white any longer.

Aria strode to him and knelt at his head. "Good riddance, Filip." With a quick twist of his skull, Aria snapped his neck then ripped his head from the body.

"Let me have it, Aria. He'll be a perfect addition." Aria looked up. Wolves fought around her, but all the vamps were lying in puddles of their own blood. Her magnificent trinity stood by, patiently watching her.

Zane looked at Aria with the dead head in her hands. His eyes sparkled. Penelope rolled her eyes. "Zane, you're insane."

Julian grunted. "I've been saying he's in *zane* for ages." He and Zane laughed at the play on spelling. The two women groaned.

A male in human form banged into Aria from behind. She turned and slashed his back, severing his spine. Aric stood in front of her when the man fell. "Thanks, Aria."

"How's it looking? All the vamps are taken care of. Do you want us to step in with you? I know you wolves don't like others interfering in your things."

ARIC SIGHED. "I appreciate the offer, but you're right about wolves and others." He looked around the scene. Even with the four's help, they were still outnumbered by Rahound's group. His brothers fought valiantly, but enemy numbers were simply overpowering. Many from both packs either lay on the blood-soaked grass or crawled away to recover. Aric hated this. Countless lives gone because of one man's greed.

He searched for Rocco, but spoke to Aria. "You're welcome to hang around. But if you help, our pack will be seen as weak and others will always be challenging. You can keep an eye on Trevan, if you like."

Aria put her nose to the air. "Why would I want to help him? He's a rogue, a man without a pack."

"More like an alpha free from any strings to do whatever he wanted, with whomever he wanted." Aric smiled. He smelled her interest in the visiting alpha. *Very* strong interest.

"Perhaps I will talk to him later, and make sure he's not double-teamed here." She quickly vanished among the melee. Aric tipped his head to the ancient three still there and headed into the brawl to salvage what he could. He glanced at his mate off to the side. She and the other women were triage for those who made it to them. They either patched them up or assisted with shifting for natural healing, then threw them back into the fight.

But the makeshift hospital was taking in more than they were shipping out. As acting alpha, it was his responsibility to decide when enough was enough and call for surrender. Again he looked around for Caleb or Rocco. Their battle results would end this mass beating his limited number pack was taking.

His mate's voice reached his ears. "Aric, we can't take anymore. You have to stop this now!" His eyes found Jordan's. This pack was as much hers as his. These were her people being injured, too. He dropped his look to his feet, then nodded. It was time.

Slamming vehicle doors pulled his attention to the small parking area not far from the fight circle. Jake, Nicole, and a slew of men hurried toward them from two passenger vans.

Aric couldn't believe it. "What the hell? How did you get here so fast?"

Jake stripped off his shirt. "We'll talk later. Now we protect the pack." Jake ran into the center ring, shifting within two steps. The men behind him followed suit. The last man in the group wasn't a happy camper, but damn he was big. Aric wondered who he was. He bet it was the cousin who challenged for the alpha spot in their pack. Shit. Would this guy take advantage of the situation and kill Nicole or Jake?

Nicole took Aric's arm as he turned to join his brothers. "Aric, where are the other women?"

He turned to her. "Where did all these guys come from?"

Nicole smiled. "The Vegas pack is well off financially, or was. They own a private jet. That's how we got here so quickly. After meeting and talking with the pack, the men wanted to help our family. They'd heard about the goodness of the Wolfe pack and wanted to fight to preserve that way of life for other packs. Alphas like their Grady Harris and Rocco Rahound, they want to eliminate."

Aric glanced over his shoulder. Tides had already started to flow their way. "Nic, your one act of bravery of standing up to Harris may save more than you will ever know." He nodded to the side. "The mates are nursing the injured. Please join them. Their task is overwhelming." With that, he jumped into the ring to find Jake.

Chapter Thirty

THE LAS VEGAS wolves were a smooth fighting machine. Packs weren't normally that trained in team combat. Aric wondered what they had gone through to see the need for this type of battle. Maybe the men were ex-military, or maybe their pack lifestyle required such knowledge just to stay alive. He hoped Jake knew what he was getting into there.

Aric had never witness Jake fight until they were in Vegas rescuing his mate Nicole from Grady Harris. His brother was vicious and efficient with his attack. Swiping claws and ninja wolf moves that Aric had never seen allowed Jake to take down everyone stupid enough to approach him. Damn. Aric was more than impressed.

Rogues fell like a swarm of bugs landing on a zapper. One of the mercenaries shifted in the middle of the field and walked toward Rahound's sidelines. "Fuck this shit. I'm not being paid enough to die for that baby penis bastard. I'm outta here." Others quickly followed. Soon the battle slowed and the Wolfe pack watched the paid fighters leave. Money can't buy loyalty. Something Rocco had yet to learn.

Aric looked around for Rocco and found him and Caleb facing off toward the top of the circle. He headed for them as those on the field made way for him. A council member called above the noise. "Do not interfere, Alpha Wolfe. The challenge remains legal until one leaves the ring."

"What about his mate's fighting for him?"

The female councilor answered. "She legally invoked her right to fight in place of her mate. Wolf law recognizes that as an equal exchange. With her mate's return, where he didn't leave the ring, the exchange was again equal. His mate has left the ring which makes her ineligible to return."

Aric gave a nod and headed for his side of the field. There was nothing he could do to help Caleb.

The two original competitors were bloody and beaten, but neither had backed down during the group melee. Both in human form, they slowly circled while regaining strength.

Rocco sneered. "Just give up, boy. I'm the alpha of this pack for a reason."

"The reason being I haven't killed you yet. No other right keeps you there. The pack despises you. They hate everything about you—from your complete biasness to allowing their children to be taken. You've failed and I'll see your reign end now." Caleb launched at Rocco, both meeting midair as wolves.

Muzzles scraped together, teeth grinding against flesh and bone. Both rolled, Caleb coming out on top, his jaws around Rocco's neck. Caleb made note of how close they were to the top of the circle. He didn't want to accidentally go out and lose on a technicality.

Wait! Caleb heard in his connection with Rocco.

What, Rocco? There is nothing I want to hear except you'll leave the circle.

You'll want to hear, more importantly see, this. Movement on the Rahound side caught Caleb's eye, but he didn't remove his death grip on his uncle's neck.

The crowd parted and two big men hauled an emaciated, bedraggled third man between them. Caleb's eyes narrowed. He was sure he wasn't seeing what his eyes told him. Then his nose proved his sight correct. He shifted into human form without thought, eyes never moving from the third man.

"Dad?"

Gasps filled the air.

Caleb felt a jab and found himself on his back. Rocco straddled Caleb's prone body, hands wrapped around his neck. He looked at his uncle, questions in his eyes.

Rocco snorted. "Yes, your pathetic daddy lives."

"How? Why?"

"The bastard crawled from the wreck, refused to die. I could've killed him, but if your mother died, I'd have no control over you. So I kept him locked in the cells below the house. Good thing I did."

"What cells?"

"Oh, you'd never guess what was found when they remodeled the alpha house. Seems when the house was built, a small prison was included, then somewhere along the way someone sealed up the entrance."

Fire shot from Caleb's eyes. "My father has been in a hole this entire time? He barely looks alive."

"We couldn't have him shifting and breaking free, now, could we?"

"You son of a bitch!" Caleb started to shift to attack.

His uncle raised a brow. "I wouldn't do that if I were you. I could have his arms torn off while you lay here and watch."

"Fuck!" Caleb screamed with frustration. "Get off me, prick." He tried to push Rocco to the side, but his uncle remained on his knees, hands locked on his throat. "I'll leave the circle. Just let him go."

Rocco smiled. "Not good enough. I want you dead and your father will join you thereafter. Or I could torture him for a few more years. Bastard always thought he was better than me."

Ellie's cry reached him. "No, Caleb. You can't die." Her tearful eyes looked at her brothers. "We have to help him. Do something."

Aric shook his head. "Ellie, there's nothing we can do to interfere with the fight or Caleb forfeits."

A gleam sparked in her eye. "Nobody said anything about interfering with the fight." With her supernatural speed, she disappeared then reappeared in front of the two men holding Caleb's father. She karate chopped the two guards in the balls before they realized what was happening and was back on her side of the battle lines with her father-in-law in tow. "I've got this, honey," she hollered out. Then in her best Mortal Kombat voice, she added, "Finish him."

Caleb grinned up at his uncle who just stared between Ellie

and his two enforcers. He saw Rocco's disbelief that she took their prisoner so easily and quickly. Still kneeling over Caleb's body, Rocco's fingers morphed into claws, ready to slash his jugular.

Caleb tightened his eight-pack stomach and drove his knees up, slamming Rocco squarely in the ass. Rocco flew forward, releasing his death grip, and landed on his back. In a heartbeat, Caleb rolled his uncle onto his stomach, pinning him in a classic wrestling hold.

Caleb snarled, "This is it, you piece of shit. Family or not, you don't deserve to live. The fear and torment you've inflicted on *my* pack is done." Caleb turned Rocco's head to stare at his father on the sidelines with the Wolfes. "Your last sight will be of a man born to guide his people. A brother you abused out of jealousy."

Caleb transformed his fingernail into a claw and held it at Rocco's neck. "Seems fitting that you die the way you intended for me without a thought." With a pluck of his finger, Caleb severed the main vessel in Rocco's neck. Blood flowed to the ground like water from a hose. "This is for my dad and mate, you piece of shit. You will die slowly, watching them remain alive. You lose, Rocco. You will never hurt my family or my pack again."

The pumping blood slowed and Rocco's body under Caleb relaxed then deflated. To ensure the horror was over, Caleb snapped the interim alpha's neck. There was no fucking way he was coming back from that.

The Wolfe clan exploded into cheers. And to Caleb's relief, so did his side of the battlefield.

Ellie ran to him and helped him off the ground. He wrapped his arms around her, giving her his weight. "It's done, sweetheart. It's finally over."

Backslaps and hugging continued among both groups. Paul Montgomery with the Vegas pack slapped Jake on the shoulder. "Well done, Alpha. You alone fight as well as our teams. We're glad to have you."

Jake squeezed Nicole's hand. "We're glad to join the pack. And I thank you for volunteering to help us out here."

"Eh," Paul started, "that's what pack does for family." He stepped toward the rental van they drove from the airport then turned. "By the way, Alpha. The challenge has been withdrawn. Guess he saw he'd lose in a fight one-on-one with you."

Behind the group, a scratchy feminine voice said, "Thank God!" All turned to see Tristan and Barbara coming from the parking area.

"Mom. Dad. They let you out?" Aric said, a grimace on his face.

His dad harrumphed. "Don't look so pleased, eldest son of mine." They walked slowly as their mom leaned on their father.

Aric looked at him, hands on his hips. "You know that's not

what I meant. My concern is that both of you are healed enough to take back alpha. It was fun for a while, but I have other things to do than stress over stuff like this right now. Why didn't you both stay overnight?"

Dad snorted. "Do you honestly think your mother would remain in bed after hearing about the shoot-out here at the corral? I don't think so."

She slapped him on the shoulder. "Sure, blame me. Who was in a hurry to get here?"

Aric looked around the parking lot in the direction they walked from. An ambulance sat not far from the triage area and the EMS team was patching up his pack members with real medicine. "Don't tell me—"

His mom stood straighter. "Yes, your father *borrowed* an ambulance and its crew as soon as I was able to stand from the bed." They watched as a technician wrapped gauze around the head of a pack member. "It was a good idea, anyway. I knew you wouldn't have professional help. You alphas and your damn sense of pride will get someone killed."

Aric's father smiled. "But not tonight, dear. Not tonight."

Two others joined the group. Caleb dragged Ellie with him and threw an arm around his father being held up by Emma and Jordan. Tristan sucked in a sharp breath. "Conly, oh my god, you're alive." He looked at his wife. "He's alive, right. I'm not seeing dead people now, am I?"

Barbara patted him on the chest. "No, dear. He appears living to me."

Tristan carefully put an arm around the frail man and gave a soft tap. "You look like shit, man. You need a lot of doctoring to get healthy again. I can't wait to hear this story." Tristan popped is chin toward the medical crew as Aric took the other side of Conly. "Let's take him to the ambulance and have them check him in. Once he regains his strength, he'll be fine."

Caleb heard his father-in-law say, "Man, do you know Glen Fry of the Eagles died? No more tequila nights for us. And that race car, I still got it in the garage..." His voice faded as more distance filled the space between Caleb and the three alphas headed toward the ambulance. Tristan was the perfect alpha and friend.

Nate joined the group. "I'm headed home to see Karla and the babies. We'll call you later this morning."

Tired and beat to hell, the others agreed that going home and talking later worked perfectly. All mates, hand in hand, shuffled toward the parking lot. Caleb heard his name called. Lael waved at him. He told Ellie to go on, he'd catch up in a moment.

"What's up, Lael?"

"I'm glad you're fine, but I knew you would be, so I wasn't

worried. Anyway, you need to keep on your toes. Don't assume there isn't danger lurking in the shadows." She glanced toward Ellie, smiled, and turned back to Caleb. "You've got your own family to watch out for now. Keep your guard up. I gotta help close down the bar, so see y'all later." She jogged away.

Caleb needed a minute for the words to set in. Then a jolt of electricity shot through him. "Lael, wait. What do you mean my own family?" She waved a hand overhead as she disappeared into the dark.

CHAPTER Thirty One

OLLIE RUBBED OIL over her skin and smiled at the scene of their bathtub. Caleb had done one hell of a job once she'd healed, trying to pamper her. There were candles all over their bathroom, a glass of her favorite wine, and soft lighting. The man knew how to work it so he could get some. She laughed at her own thoughts. Like he'd have to do much to get her to give it up. Being in heat had him doing all kinds of things to be at her side. Down to getting her spaghetti whenever she pouted.

He even thought he'd gotten away with secretly hiring

someone to build them a small cabin while a brand new alpha house was constructed. For so long, she hadn't believed this could be possible. Him and her, together and not having to worry about Rocco.

She left the bathroom with her glass of wine in hand and stood at the open doorway for a second, waiting to watch her husband's reaction. He was busy fixing flowers on a dresser. Flowers that had not been there before. He'd gotten to know how much she loved tulips, especially the blue ones. He'd made it his business to find them for her.

It took a second before the breeze from the open window carried her scent to him, and he stopped and turned to face her.

She'd waited so long for this. Them, alone in their own home. Even if this was a temporary place, she was finally with him.

"How are you feeling?" He licked his lips.

She saw the brightness of his animal light in his eyes, roaming down her naked body. "I feel like you owe me something."

He raised his brows. "Oh yeah? What's that, sweetheart?"

"A mating."

He gripped the dresser hard. She wondered when the wood would splinter from the force he was clearly putting on it. Heck, his knuckles had turned white. "I don't know if now's the right time, Ellie. With everything you've been through—"

She shook her head and took soft steps toward him, her eyes never leaving his. "No, this is where you're mistaken, husband." She stopped in front of him and raked her nails down his shirt, bunching the material and sliding her hands under it to feel his hot, muscled chest. "I didn't just spend hours shaving for nothing."

He barked a chuckle at her pout. "Hours shaving? What, do you have a Brazilian rainforest for legs?"

She tugged his shirt off and gripped his shoulders. "It will be okay, baby," she teased. "I'll prove it to you."

He leaned down and meshed their lips together into a kiss so hot, so raw, it melted her from the inside. She pulled away, licking his jaw and that short beard that drove her absolutely crazy. She moved down his torso, placing kisses and hungry bites on his abs and down his hip. On her knees, she got a chance to caress his cock with her fingers. The gentle massage got a groan out of him. He stood still, his body tense, almost vibrating.

"Ah, Ellie. You know just what to do to get me to lose my mind. Do it," he urged, sliding his fingers into her hair and gripping her strands hard. "Suck my dick."

She wrapped a hand around his length as her head lowered to cover the head of his cock with her lips. He was velvety soft, but steel hard and smoking hot. With a flick of her tongue, she licked off the bead of moisture at the tip, moaning. She loved the way he groaned and thrust his hips forward.

"Ah, baby girl. Open wide and take me. I want to see your spit coating my dick," he grunted as he urged his length into her mouth. "I want to see it disappear into your mouth." He gripped her hair tighter. "That's it, sweetheart. Let me watch my cock fuck your beautiful lips."

She sucked him deeply, slowly pulling her head back and leaving a trail of wetness over his dick. Then she sucked him in again, using one hand to fondle his balls and the other to grab his ass. Warmth curled in her belly and traveled to her sex, dripping down her legs.

He grunted and groaned, pushing her face into his thrusts. She brought a hand down between her folds and played with herself. Her body tightened as she sucked him harder and faster.

He tugged her off his cock and took a step back. "Keep going. I want to watch you."

She sat back on the rug, her legs wide open, and continued to finger her pussy while meeting his gaze. "Caleb, I need—"

He grasped his slick cock. "I know what you need. I have it right here and as soon as I see you come, I'll fuck you for all the times we haven't been together, baby."

She pressed at her clit, rubbing wet fingers over it and strumming it hard. Her breaths became choppy. She tugged a nipple with her other hand and felt the orgasm gathering at her core.

"That's it, baby. Come. Let go." He continued jerking off and lowered to place his cock by her mouth. She sucked him and fingered herself faster.

"Ah, sweetheart. I'm going to fill your pretty mouth with my cum. You want that, don't you, Ellie?"

She moaned, his dick deeply down her throat and the sweet taste of his seed filling her mouth. He pushed hard, coming in her mouth and grunting with each jerk of his hips.

She pressed harder on her clit, her stomach went tight and her muscles tensed before they went lax. Loud moans tore from her throat as the orgasm flowed through her.

She was still feeling it take a hold of her body when he put her over the edge of the bed and took her in one quick, hard drive. The movement pushed a new climax to soar in her. She grasped the sheets in her fists, her ass pushing out to meet each of his thrusts.

The orgasm ripped through her hard, leaving her shaking and gasping for air. He continued his hard thrusts until he became stiff and roared by her ear, his canines embedding in her shoulder as he filled her with his seed. The animal came close to the skin. She sensed it. The fingers holding her hip had turned to claws.

"We're not done yet," he said in an almost unintelligible growl.

With a gruff groan, he pulled out of her, went to the bedside table and returned, a bottle of lube in his hand. She grinned at what was coming. In order to be fully mated, she needed to take him in every way possible. Cool liquid landed on her ass, dripped between her cheeks and down to her pussy.

He slid human fingers into her ass, working her hole the same way he always did. She moaned at the spike of fire in her pussy. She whimpered at how good it felt to push into his fingers, to feel him add a second and increase the wide thrusts to get her ready for him.

"Fuck, sweetheart. You have such a gorgeous ass. So pale and perfect. The exact shape of a heart. My fucking heart."

She found herself rocking, moaning with each wiggle of her hips.

"I wish I could eat your pussy and fuck your ass at the same time," he growled.

"I don't know how you'd accomplish that. I love your flexibility but I don't want to see you broken in half." She grinned into the bedding. Her mate was one horny wolf she'd never get enough of. "Fuck me, already."

His fingers came out and were replaced with his cock. He pushed in slow at first, taking his time to ensure she was ready. She was more than ready. She shoved back, embedding his cock into her ass to the hilt. God dammit, that felt so good! Better than good. It was like floating in a sea of absolute pleasure.

She slipped a hand under her to rub over her wet folds. Then she pressed hard at her clit. He thrusted and retreated with quick, harsh drives. Every time he slammed into her ass, she tapped at her clit, sending a combination of pleasure and pain to her core. Another thrust and she tapped harder.

She gasped for air, her body slick with sweat and her muscles shaking from the nearing climax.

"Fuck, Ellie. I love you so damn much, baby girl." He went deep, balls deep, and retreated. "I will never want another woman the way I want you. You're meant for me. Only me."

She tapped her clit again. The nubbin ached and hardened with her furious taps. "I love you, too," she managed to get out.

Another thrust, this one faster. He increased in speed and she sensed his impending orgasm nearing. "Forever, sweetheart."

One final tap and she squeezed hard at his cock and let her body shake with the overwhelming sensations raking her body. He howled loudly, his cock pushing its way into her tight anal muscles and stopping. His canines embedded in her other shoulder, deeper this time and held her still as he shook above her, filling her ass with his cum.

It took some really long fucking moments before either could breathe normally or move at all. They'd stayed as they were, with him in her ass and her body still twitching from how hard she'd come. He licked her shoulders and kissed her gently over her already healed wounds.

"My Ellie. Always mine."

When he pulled out of her and she was able to turn over, she straddled him and curled her arms around his neck. "We belong to each other. Mates. Fated. There's never been any doubt."

"Never, baby girl. I love you."

She grinned and kissed him. Loving Caleb had been her whole life from the moment she'd laid eyes on him so long ago. Now she knew with enough time and perseverance, anything was possible. Even the love she thought might be lost in a never-ending war.

Epilogue

CALEB STOOD IN the backyard of the newly built Rahound alpha house complex. Too many bad memories and too much blood had flowed through the old house. This was a fresh beginning for a new way of pack living.

And what better way to show that than celebrating their new alpha's marriage. Yes, everyone knew Caleb and Ellie had married quietly. So this renewal of vows was to show the world how much he loved Ellie. And how much Nathan loved Karla, Jake loved Nicole, and Mason loved Emma.

Hundreds had gathered from both Rahound and Wolfe

families and packs for the grandest ceremony of love they had seen.

Aria and Trevan sat together. Each tried to look uninterested in the other, but were obviously leaning toward each other. Caleb was surprised, yet, he wasn't. Trevan's horrific past with vampires had devastated him completely. Maybe Aria was meant to get him through that and healed. They would be an interesting couple to keep an eye on.

Jaxon, Aric's friend from Golden Falls, had become a good comrade. He and his men helped a great amount in taking out rogues Rocco brought in to take over the Wolfe pack. Jaxon leaned against a pole, flirting with Letty. Nicole was so going to kick his ass if she saw him hitting on her little sister. Glad not to be him.

Then there was the Central pack council and the beta couple. After explaining to the council that Mason was married, but their marriage certificate was delayed due to administrative issues within the office, the Central pack had no problems. They thought if one of the boys were available, they would push for a union to make the change as smooth as possible for the pack. They invited both Mason and his mate to visit.

When Mason and Emma arrived, Mason understood why the council didn't think an unmated brother would object to marrying the alpha bitch. The woman was stunningly beautiful, but didn't hold a candle to his Ellie. Caleb needed to ask Mason if he and Emma had decided to stay with Central and help them get back on track.

Caleb knew those two would make a wonderful alpha couple for the pack. He hoped Central didn't have a history as dark as the Rahounds had. But even if they did, they had strong leaders to get them through.

Thinking about the brothers, he realized that each had their own pack now. Except for Nate. But he and Karla wanted to stay close to Grandma Barbara for support, and nightly dinners Nate so elegantly mentioned. Caleb had never seen an alpha family like the Wolfes. He was glad Tristan was around to be his role model. But now his father was back.

With Rocco and his enforcers gone, Caleb and Ellie, with the help of his father, had brought the pack together several nights a week for mutual healing and support. Stories were shared, faults where forgiven, and friendships renewed. The completion of the Rahound compound was the final expulsion of the old regime.

The compound housed entertainment venues, recreation for children, and a facility large enough for the entire pack to come together when the need arose. Educational courses for adults and children were supported by volunteers, as well as job placement opportunities within the pack and local communities.

Oh, and Caleb couldn't forget the Olympic-sized community pool and water slides behind the alpha house. One hundred percent of the children voted on that requirement. Who was Caleb to ignore mass majority rule? Only a few yards to the side, the crystal clear water sparkled like millions of diamonds floating on the current.

Happy faces glowed with warm sunlight. Three adorable babies, two dressed in tiny tuxes and one in a pearly white dress, were passed around, each eager to have a bite of what their current holder had to eat. Well, until it came to the broccoli dipped in ranch dressing, then they were happy to just lick off the white stuff.

Grandma and the two grandpas helped the nanny load the triplets inside the house where they could safely, and quietly, sit at the floor to ceiling windows and watch the goings-on. Papa Nate made a face at them and they giggled behind the glass.

"Caleb!" He glanced from the makeshift stage to his beautiful Ellie dolled up in her mother's wedding dress with a slight alteration that allowed for her little peanut bump. "Let's get the show on the road. I'm hungry."

"That's right, honey. But you're always hungry now."

"Don't make me come up there and hurt you."

Caleb winked at her. "Of course not, sweetheart." He picked

up the mic and tapped the top. "Hey, everyone. It's time to start." He wiped his upper lip. "Good thing this is just a renewal, or you'd think I was nervous. Fortunately, there was a restroom nearby where we did get hitched."

Ellie added, "I won't tell anyone how you stayed in there until two minutes before you said 'I do.'" Those paying attention laughed.

He grinned with a slight pink tinge. "Yeah, but be glad I could walk out on my own. The guy before me leaned on his best man to get through the restroom door."

All the mates and brothers had taken their seats in the first row and most others had found a chair also.

"Welcome, everybody, to my and Ellie's renewal of vows with specials guests, her brothers and mates, who also married too quietly for their mother's preference. Aric and Jordan got a pass because they already did this, but technically they did get married before they got married again. To each other, of course." Another round of laughter.

Ellie glanced at her watch and mouthed *I'm hungrier* to him.

"Right, moving on. Ellie and I would like to take this moment to say a few things before we get to the renewals." He held a hand out to her. "Sweetheart, you want to come up here, too?" She made her way with applause from the crowd. Caleb noticed the red cheeks she sported. She was as used to be the center of attention as he was.

"We want to thank all of you not only for joining us today, but for believing and trusting in us to put this pack back on track. We've endured a lot, and it's time to take off the last bandages and get to living normal lives again." Applause punctuated his decree.

"Ellie and I promise to always put pack needs before our own and our door will always be open no matter the time. Just call if you're coming over after eleven."

Ellie leaned toward the mic. "Or before seven a.m. These toes don't see daylight before then."

Someone from the crowd hollered, "Wait a few more months and that'll change." Ellie placed a hand on her growing stomach and laughed.

Caleb continued. "There are a few people here I'd like to recognize because they've played such an important part in both our lives." He glanced at the second row of seats. "My mom and dad, and Ellie's mom and dad, Tristan and Barbara."

A standing ovation roared. After a long minute, Caleb went on. "Both our parents taught us right from wrong, and how to give unconditional love. They showed us how to be good alphas and even better people. Ellie and I hope we can be as good at parenting as they are."

Ellie leaned over again. "If not, we're sending all the rugrats to the grandparents until they turn thirty." Laughter came from the audience.

"Also, for those who don't know, my dad is retiring as soon as he and I get everything wrapped up. He's thinking about moving to the same area Mom lives." His mother's face flushed red. "Was I supposed to keep that quiet—"

NATE'S ATTENTION WAS pulled from Caleb. Around the corner of the house ran a pup dressed in a tux, in his mouth a steak the size of his head. Behind him was the catering chef, shouting and waving a spoon over her head. Next, two pups, one in a tux and one in a pearly white dress, rounded the corner. The bedraggled nanny, trying to catch up, bumped into the table display of Jordan's new book *Scent of a Mate*. Bookmarkers, pens, key chains, and other swag spilled along the grass.

Nate and Karla whipped around to look through the windows. Nope, no babies sitting inside. They groaned.

The pup with the steak jumped on people's laps and snaked through hands reaching out and grabbing. Seated ladies launched to their feet, knocking chairs over, not wanting to get steak juice on their dresses. Others raced after the young'uns to help the nanny.

Nate heard a familiar yippy squeal and turned to see a little tail sticking out of a white dress disappear over the ledge of the pool. He was on the other side of the stage and into the pool before Karla knew he was gone. He surfaced with a drenched rat, white dress clinging, licking his face.

Someone whispered, "Isn't that why babies aren't supposed to shift until they're older?"

Elsewhere in the crowd, a hand shot up and Lael's voice rang out. "Sorry about that. My bad. We'll talk later."

A dripping Nate handed over a dripping, lolling, wide-eye, tail-wagging happy camper to her nanny. The little girl yipped, making everyone in the crowd say, "Ahhhh, how cute." A man and a lady brought the other two tail-waggers over. The chef stomped past with a half-chewed steak in hand.

AFTER EVERYONE WAS settled once more, Caleb's dad, Conly, took the stage and mic. He looked around at the packs as tears came to his eyes. "This is a sight I truly believed I would never see again. So much has changed, yet, so much hasn't. As Caleb mentioned, I'm retiring soon. I have complete trust and faith in my son to lead you all back into happiness and normalcy.

"I'm so sorry you had to endure what you did with that

madman. But I'm not up here to talk about the old, I'm up here to bring in the new." He looked at the front row. "Would you all take your places?"

The Wolfe brothers and their mates stood before the stage, Caleb and Ellie in the center.

Conly continued. "Since this a renewal, I get to see my son marry. And I can tell him what not to say that'll get him into trouble later." He winked at his son and moved the mic away. "Just joking, kid. Sort of."

He cleared his throat, wiping a tear with his finger. "Since there are so many couples marrying, they decided to come up with one vow," he pulled a folded sheet of paper from his pants pocket, "a rather long vow." He unfolded and glanced at the paper, his head tilting down as he scanned the typing.

"I understand why this ceremony is this year and not last year. If the men had to come up with this on their own, it would be *next* year." He straightened the paper. "Okay, guys, I'll read to the audience while you look into the prettiest eyes you've ever seen and let your heart speak to her.

"I will care for and protect you, nurture you, and support you, and tell you your butt is perfect in every dress and adore everything about you.

I promise to love you tirelessly through perfect times and the merely fabulous times.

I promise to leave you alone one week every month, for my sanity and yours.

I promise to try to always put the toilet seat down.

I promise to try to remember to put my dirty clothes in the hamper and replace the toilet paper when the roll is empty.

I promise to use plenty of lube before trying to poke things in your bellybutton, no promise about your ears, though.

In the presence of our beloved family and friends, I offer you my solemn vow to be your godlike partner and lover. In good times and bad and in joy as well as sorrow, I give you my heart, my love, my soul.

I love you, now and forever."

Conly wiped his cheek. "Boys, that was beautiful. I truly believe you wrote this all by yourselves." He chuckled with the group. He folded that paper, slipped it into his pocket, then slid another sheet out of his other pocket. "Okay, ladies. Let's see what you've got to say. You boys, listen up. You've already said yes. It's too late now." He smiled. "I'm on a roll here. Maybe I'll take up a gig as a stand-up comedian." Several in the audience groaned.

His brows lowered. "Fine, maybe not. I'll stay and do birthday parties for the kiddies. Think they'll understand when I talk about payphones at the corner 7-11 store I drove to in my Pinto?" Those under the age of thirty looked confused. "That's what I thought."

Caleb cleared his throat. "Come on, Dad. Ellie's eyeing the buffet table, and she won't let me keep her waiting."

"Okay, son. I haven't talked in over ten years. Just trying to make up for all that time right now." He mouthed, *kidding, I love you.* "Ladies, gaze into the most handsome face you've ever seen and say, "Yup, it's too late." He flicked the paper in his hand. "No, really, here we go.

"I promise to laugh with you, cry with you, and grow with you.

I promise to support your dreams and to respect our differences, and to love you and be by your side through all the days and nights of our lives.

I promise to create and support a family with you, in a household filled with laughter, patience, understanding, and love. I vow not just to grow old together, but to grow together.

We shall bear together whatever trouble and sorrow life may lay upon us, and we shall share together whatever good and joyful things life may bring us.

With these words, and all the words of my heart, I re-marry you and bind my life to yours.

"Grooms, you may kiss your brides. Karla, you can kiss your wet husband."

There wasn't a dry eye in the crowd. The love shared between mates was what every child dreamed of having. Ellie's mother beamed with pure joy, seeing all her children happily married. That was until Ellie decided to end the ceremony with, "Let's eat!"

ABOUT THE AUTHOR
NEW YORK TIMES & USA TODAY BESTSELLER

Hi! I'm Milly Taiden. I love to write sexy stories featuring fun, sassy heroines with curves and growly alpha males with fur. My books are a great, quick way to satisfy your craving for paranormal romantic comedies with lots of romance, heat, and happily ever afters.

    I live in Florida with my hubby, our boy child, and our little fur babies "Needy Speedy" and "Stormy." Yes, I am aware I'm bossy, and I am seriously addicted to shoe shopping and Dunkin' Donuts coffee.

    Hey, I love to meet new readers, so come sign up for my newsletter and check out my Facebook page. We always have lots of fun stuff going on there.

SIGN UP FOR MILLY'S NEWSLETTER FOR LATEST NEWS!
http://eepurl.com/pt9q1

FIND OUT MORE ABOUT MILLY TAIDEN HERE:

Email: millytaiden@gmail.com
Website: www.millytaiden.com
Facebook: www.facebook.com/millytaidenpage
Twitter: www.twitter.com/millytaiden

If you liked this story, you might also enjoy the following by Milly Taiden:

Sassy Mates Series

Scent of a Mate *Sassy Mates Book One*

A Mate's Bite *Sassy Mates Book Two*

Unexpectedly Mated *Sassy Mates Book Three*

A Sassy Wedding *Short 3.7*

The Mate Challenge *Sassy Mates Book Four*

Sassy in Diapers *Short 4.3*

Fighting for her Mate *Book Five*

Federal Paranormal Unit

Wolf Protector *Book One*

Dangerous Protector *Book Two*

Unwanted Protector *Book Three*

Black Meadow Pack

Sharp Change *Black Meadows Pack Book One*

Caged Heat *Black Meadows Pack Book Two*

Paranormal Dating Agency

Twice the Growl *Book One*

Geek Bearing Gifts *Book Two*

The Purrfect Match *Book Three*

Curves 'Em Right *Book Four*

Tall, Dark and Panther *Book Five*

The Alion King *Book Six*

There's Snow Escape *Book Seven*

Scaling Her Dragon *Book Eight*

In The Roar *Book Nine*

Scrooge Me Hard – *Holiday Short*

Bearfoot and Pregnant – *Book Ten*

All Kitten Aside – *Book Eleven - Coming Soon*

The Bear King Series

The Bear King's Captive *Book One*

The Bear King's Revenge *Book Two - Coming Soon*

The Bear King's Queen *Book Three - Coming Soon*

FUR-ocious Lust - Bears

Fur-Bidden *Book One*

Fur-Gotten *Book Two*

Fur-Given Book *Three*

FUR-ocious Lust - Tigers

Stripe-Tease *Book Four*

Stripe-Search *Book Five*

Stripe-Club *Book Six*

Raging Falls

Miss Taken *Book One*

Miss Matched *Book Two*

Miss Behaved *Book Three- Coming Soon*

Printed in Great Britain
by Amazon